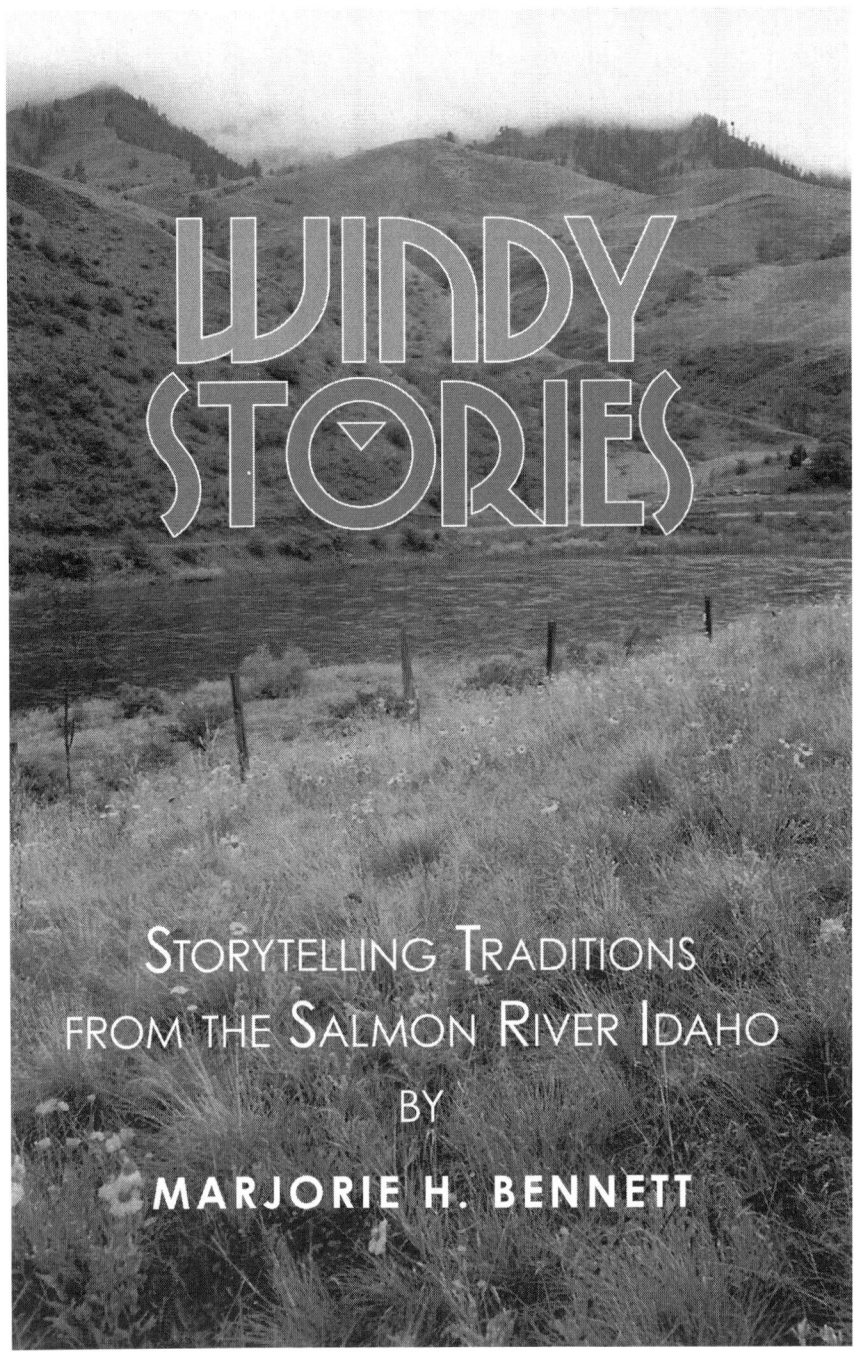

WINDY STORIES

Storytelling Traditions from the Salmon River Idaho

By

MARJORIE H. BENNETT

iUniverse, Inc.
New York   Bloomington

WINDY STORIES
Storytelling Traditions from the Salmon River Idaho

iUniverse books may be ordered through booksellers or by contacting:

iUniverse
1663 Liberty Drive
Bloomington, IN 47403
www.iuniverse.com
1-800-Authors (1-800-288-4677)

ISBN: 978-0-595-51798-5 (sc)
ISBN: 978-0-595-62037-1 (ebk)

Printed in the United States of America

iUniverse rev. date: 03/16/2009

A little taste for the reader of *Windy Stories*.
The stories in this work have been transcribed in poetic format to
suggest the pioneer narrators' speech patterns.

"Vandenburg in the Tree"
Del Ringer, September 1975

There was an old fellow,
Vandenburg.
Here was a family in there,
by name of Lockhorn,
and she was big old gal.
She caught him going across
her land one day.

And she got after him
with an ax blade.
She was going to tell him
what she was going to do to him.

Well, he climbed a tree,
figurin' he was safe up there.

She kept a-yellin'.
Thought she'd abuse him
into coming down.
She'd say:

"Come on down from there,
you old billy goat, you!"

He had chin whiskers.
Said:
"Oh, no,
I'm too brave a man for that."

She kept a-hollerin'.
Saw the girls a-comin' out.
Said:
"Bring me the axe."
She cut down the tree
with the old man in it.

She went in the house after that,
and the old man crawled
down the tree.

(Motif K 983.1: "Tree cut
down to get victim in top")

Acknowledgements

Grateful acknowledgment is made to the following for permission to print material previously published:

Pacific Northwest Forum for material revised and expanded from *Pacific Northwest Forum*, Volume X, Number 2, Spring 1985, pp. 21–27, and Number 3/4, Summer/ Fall 1985, pp. 37–45.

Northwest Folklore for material revised and expanded from *Northwest Folklore*, Volume 7, Number 1, and Fall 1988, pp.16–29.

"Del Ringer and his Tales of Salmon River." *Traditional Storytelling Today*, edited by Margaret Read MacDonald, Fitzroy Dearborn, Chicago, IL, 1999, 403–407.

I wish to express appreciation to Dr. Sandra Stahl of the University of Indiana, Folklore Institute, Del Skeels and members of my graduate committee at the University of Washington, and Dr. Margaret Read MacDonald for their encouragement and help with this project.

I am grateful to my children, Robin, Kristin, and Paul Bennett, who have been my support team through the years.

Finally, I wish to thank my informants and their families, Carolyn Frei and the Grangeville Bicentennial Museum, and all my friends along the Salmon who have so willingly shared their tales and photos with me. They made it a joy to collect and share these "windy stories." As Gus Carlson said in 1985, "Boy, them old-timers sure told some windy stories."

Foreword By Dr. Kenneth Clarke

Now heading into my 93rd year I am comfortable with admitting that I have forgotten some of the details of some significant events. One of those events was the surprise arrival of Marjorie Bennett's booklet of Windy Tales told by Del Ringer, my uncle. She had abstracted these tales from the much larger collection which she is now publishing. And this is my Foreword to that very ambitious work.

The "surprise arrival" mentioned above contained enough commentary to tell me that Marjorie Bennett had targeted the oral literature of an isolated community, and that this rich material had been available to me as it had been to her. She had learned of my occupation as a folklorist, and my family relationship with Del Ringer, and she was kind enough to mail a copy to me.

Her little booklet is now out of my reach, for I sent it along to one of my former teaching colleagues as it was my practice to do after I retired and found that my to-large library was a burden rather than a convenience. However I, was quick to respond with thanks for her gift with thanks for her gift, and I evidently added my slight feeling of chagrin for failing to recognize what had been readily available to me. I had chose, rather, to take off for Kentucky where I settled in a very traditional rural area, bought a small abandoned farm, and tried to become one of the folk who finally became my neighbors and sometimes tried to stump me by bringing me some object dug out of the old smokehouse , to say with a grin, "Betcha you don't know what this is fer."

Now for the Foreword: Marjorie Bennett surprised me by sending a remarkably hefty package containing the finished manuscript of *WINDY STORIES*. Briefly put, she has dedicated her efforts for many years to this impressive collection, taking her camera and tape recorder to that sparely settled Salmon River country in Western Idaho having a focus on the area the local people named White Bird. Actually one was go over the pass to Grangeville to get a high school education. White Bird offers only grade school, or so it was when my mother, Violet Harrah, went to Grangeville to work for board and room so that she could attend high school. She stuck it out for two year , then returned to the homestead which she had grown up with her seven sisters and four brothers.

One can understand why the Bennett collection was so long in the making by consulting her bibliography. She started early in her eagerness to collect well by picking up on the hints she listed in her bibliography: Books by such well-known folklorists as Abrams, Bauman, Dundes, Brunvand, Dorson, just to name a few. As the project grew so did her motivation to return to her informants repeatedly over the years.

This is an impressive publication, long in its preparation and deep in its analysis of the relationship of the story-tellers to their setting, it history, to each other. Students first taking to the field might do well to have a look at this unusual collection. It seems as complete as one ambitious collector could make it.

As other collectors have tried to do elsewhere. Bennett worked out her own page format to improve the presentation of the informant's dramatic style. The recitation is presented much as poetry is traditionally presented on the page with wide margins to allow variation in line-length giving more hints about pacing. Volume (sometimes explosive, as in the performance of Del Ringer) spaced out in italics. These techniques were quite adequate in my reading.

Having read the manuscript with much interest, I had made these paragraphs of descriptive comment, mostly slanted toward the prospective scholarly readers, and turned to the computer to finish writing a rather self-centered approval. It so happened that my neighbor, a retired domestic school teacher, dropped in on some domestic errand, and learning that I was at the computer, excused me, but asked to be allowed to remain in the living room where she had gotten interested in the manuscript which had been lying nearby. Somewhat later she started on her own rave review. She could not, she said recall any recently acquired book that so quickly grabbed her interest.

At that moment I suddenly realized that I had been overlooking all along the commercial possibilities but had tried to show my "professional distance." She commented on all those years of work, borrowing rare photographs from the museum, all that driving to and from the Salmon River Country, all that tracking down those great informants – she should have been the one to write this foreword.

Every relative of the pioneer settlers whose photographs appear in his page would be likely prospects as future readers. History buff will see unusual slants on historic events in the unadorned narration of those children of the homesteaders of Idaho, for example, the sorry plight of the Indians as recalled by the descendants of the settlers comes to mind. This book has a place in every public library.

Contents

Part One
Del Ringer and his Stories

Chapter One:
Introduction

Them old guys sure told some windy stories. I wish I
had wrote down the sayings of these old timers.

—Gus Carlson, August 31, 1985

As long as I can remember, I have loved listening to entertaining stories
about life long ago, or as Gus Carlson called them, "windy stories."
As a child, I often begged my father and mother to tell me how it
was in the "old days," when they were young. I enjoyed hearing about
simple little incidents like how my mother made hollyhock dolls to
play with in the tiny city garden of her family's brownstone mansion
on Monroe Street in old Chicago, or how she begged slivers of ice
from the iceman's wagon. I was thrilled when my father told how he
and his little sister ran for home as fast as their legs would carry them
when they met gypsies in the woodlands near Kansas City, Missouri,
or how his grandmother back in Pennsylvania tore up all the bed sheets
to nurse both the wounded Confederates and Yankees after the battle
of Gettysburg. These were the greatest bedtime stories as far as I was
concerned. I liked hearing them again and again. As an adult, this
pleasure in hearing real life stories did not pale for me. In fact, it seemed
that wherever I went, my ears would perk up whenever someone began
relating remarkable "windy" stories about personal experiences in the
past. I began taping interviews with these storytellers. Something inside

3

told me these stories should be saved. I did not know then that this is what folklorists do.

About 1973, I realized that what I had been doing in this story-collecting hobby was acting as an amateur folklorist. I decided it was time to learn how to collect folklore properly. I searched out whatever courses I could find pertaining to folklore at the University of Washington. At that time, there was no Department of Folklore or Folklife. In one of my first courses, an introduction to folklore course taught by Dr. Del Skeels, I fortunately paid close attention to a chance remark made by a fellow student, Laurie Hallowell. I didn't know it then, but this remark led to a very important encounter in my life. Laurie told me about her great uncle, Del Ringer, who lived in North Bend, Washington, a logging community about thirty miles east of Seattle. She said that he told stories that, "somebody ought to get." Shortly thereafter, on a whim, I called on Del and Martha Ringer and began tape recording his stories. I knew I was meeting a man who had a way with words when he introduced me to his wife Martha, saying, "She is a good old wagon, even if her wheels do squeak." He cast his spell with his storying from the first moment. I was hooked with the following story about a character he knew in his youth, Old Jewett.

"Jewett's Red Whiskers"

Old Jewett had red whiskers,
red bristles
sticking out all over his face.
He'd go anyplace.
He come to one place.
There was a woman
had a little daughter.
She put a meal on the tablecloth.
The little girl stood at the door
behind the kitchen and dining room.
Said
"Mama, Mama,
them whiskers open up
and the food disappears."

In 1976, I took a job teaching high school English and speech in the same community where the Ringers lived, North Bend, Washington. When my students complained they had nothing to write or talk about, I urged them to use interesting stories that they had heard from their family, neighbors, and friends, or from their own life experiences. Soon they were intriguing me with all kinds of wonderful tales like the one about an old fellow who knew Sitting Bull, or a guy who had actually seen a Sasquatch. I asked some of my students to take me with them to meet some of the colorful characters they talked about. I began collecting stories of these North Bend narrators, most of whom were loggers. The task I chose for myself was to gather the stories of these North Bend loggers into a collection.

I continued to visit with Del Ringer and found him by far my most interesting narrator and the one to whom I was drawn to return. From 1973 to 1982, I returned to tape record his stories on five occasions. In addition, his wife Martha intrigued me with a remark that another of their nieces, Mary Auvil, had made tape recordings of him back in the 1960s when the whole family was together on a fishing trip. I wrote to Mary who shared with me her transcript of those stories. Eventually, I had a collection of some forty distinct stories that Del had told and retold over a period of many years. I realized that these were well-honed, consistent stories in his repertoire and not just random conversational bits. I was taken by his storytelling style. I was curious to determine what made it so special.

A puzzling surprise was that Del never told any stories about North Bend and his life in logging. He had lived there for thirty-six years and had worked for the Weyerhauser Lumber Company for some twenty-six years before retiring. Rather, his engaging stories were about his youthful years ranching at the turn of the century along the Salmon River in Idaho where his family members were homesteaders. He seemed quite a unique teller, not sharing much in common with the other narrators I was collecting in the community of North Bend. I wondered what was so special about that Salmon River country and why it had such a strong hold on him that it remained the topic of his stories after all these years.

In 1985, curiosity finally got the best of me. I had to see the setting of his tales for myself. I wanted to see if there might even be other storytellers like him over in Idaho in the locale of his stories. Since he had been gone some fifty years from the Salmon River country, I wasn't really optimistic that I would find storytellers like him there, but even so, I thought at least I could better visualize the settings of his stories if I made a trip to the area.

In 1985 over Labor Day weekend, my teenaged son, Paul, and I set out for a few days camping in the areas of Riggins, Slate Creek, and White Bird, Idaho, the areas Del had mentioned most often. Our first night we stopped at Stinkers, a little store in Riggins, and casually inquired if there was anybody around who told stories about the area. That was the beginning of our adventure that led us on from one teller to another. There was a young man at the counter who said we ought to meet, Delbert Wicks, "a great talker." He called Delbert and asked permission for us to stop by in the morning. Bright and early the next day we visited with Delbert Wicks. We were not disappointed. He was a great talker. After that, Delbert then took us to meet Gay and Ralph Robie. The Robies introduced us to Ralph's sister, Alice Mahurin, through whom we met her son, Ron Mahurin. The Mahurins suggested I talk to Gus Carlson.

The weekend went by much too quickly. It was with regret that I returned to North Bend for the first day of school. I could hardly wait to start transcribing the stories. All of these people had proven to be storytellers who had agreed to let me record and share their narratives. In addition, I later realized that Del's wife, Martha, and her sisters had also grown up along the Salmon at the same time as Del and the narrators I had met in the Salmon River country. I decided to tape record them as well.

Obviously, my project had to change. For the time being I abandoned the idea of collecting North Bend logger stories. I turned instead to trying to see what relationship Del Ringer's storytelling might have with that of the other narrators I had met in Idaho and in his family. I was curious. Could there be a community storytelling style of which they all partook? My gut feeling was that they seemed to all be operating out of a common tradition. I reasoned that once I got all the stories transcribed and looked at them carefully perhaps answers would be revealed to me.

As I delved into folklore studies, I learned that narrators like Del Ringer practice their creativity in the structure or frame provided by their local culture. Barry Toelken, who discusses folkloric traditions as variations in time and space of cultural premises, says:

> Tradition is here understood to mean ... those pre-existing culture specific materials and options that bear upon the performer more heavily than do his or her own personal tastes and talents. We recognize that in the use of tradition that such matters as content and style have been for the most part passed on, but not invented by the performer.[1]

Similarly, Walter Ong writes:

> The performance of the oral narrator or singer is very little determined by conscious intent: the formulas and the themes—the traditions—control him more than he controls them.[2]

In the formulation of my thoughts about storytelling style, the theories of Munro Edmonson were also influential. Edmonson views style as features of folklore, which develop in a particular contextual situation, i.e., the style of an individual grows out of the particular context of communication in one period and area. Edmunson says:

> For purposes of cultural analysis individual style may be viewed as variations on culturally given themes. Ogden Nash could not have used rhymes had he been an American Indian Bard of the fourteenth century. What gives form to individual styles is the result of selection from pre-existing cultural ideas. Styles are established within the individual and among individuals with a shared background.[3]

Thus, it appeared to me that most likely each individual storyteller has a style of storytelling that is unique to an extent, but that also partakes of shared community style.

An individual's style then would consist of the features that an individual consistently selects from the available cultural repertoire and combines in his or her own unique way. Of course there would be features that are common to many tellers, but the stamp of the individual would lie in the selection of patterns of expression that are consistently preferred. I knew that with Del Ringer I had a selection of repeated stories that could definitely show the features that he persisted in using over a long period time, and that by examining them, I ought to be able determine quite clearly his preferred style of telling.

Then came the question, what features should I examine? We have all had the experience of listening to several people tell about a common experience. One teller will make it a real event for us. Another simply recounts an explanation of what happened in what order, probably very accurate but not something remarkable or very interesting that we would ask for again. What is the difference?

It might lie in the vocabulary chosen and the way the teller puts words together. I decided to look first of all at features at the surface level of word choice and grammar. Though I realized that broad regional dialect patterns would be involved here, I still knew that individuals show definite preferences at this level.

It might lie in the choices a narrator makes about how to frame the story. Like the author of written tale, the oral storyteller has to select details to use in the story to bring it to life. Does he decide to tell with lots of colorful descriptive phrases and use literary devices like metaphors, similes, repetition, or irony? Would we learn inner thoughts of characters or perhaps hear them quoted in direct or indirect discourse? What knowledge would the teller make us privilege to that the characters presented didn't know? It seemed to me that decisions made about this framing of the story would be the place where the artistry of the individual teller would be apparent, or perhaps even obviously lacking. I also wanted to look at oral presentational techniques of the tellers, such as vocal techniques and gestures.

Finally, the magic of a story just might lie in how effectively the story makes its point.[4] Recounting of what I bought on my latest trip to the grocery does not make a story. We tell stories to make a point about our beliefs about life that will be interesting to others, and to capture their attention much more persuasively than just flat out saying that this is what we believe. Personal stories act as little rhetorical strategies for tellers. Thus, I decided my final task would be to look at underlying themes, topics, and attitudes in these stories to see what personal statements lay there.

As I set out to make sense of all these stories I had collected, my plan was to first determine Del's preferences in these matters, and then I would ascertain if the tellers in Idaho and in his family might share storytelling techniques with Del Ringer. If I was successful in identifying shared features, these would represent the community traditional style of which Del Ringer was a product.

In the end to my delight, even though Del Ringer had left Idaho some fifty years ago, his stories represented clear regional storytelling characteristics revealed in the community traditions of the Salmon River region where he spent his formative years. All the narratives I recorded vividly projected the flavor of the region, yet, as I suspected, each narrator presented narratives in a somewhat unique personal style full of idiosyncrasies reflecting the personality of each individual. I found the twin forces of individual creativity through variation, as well as cultural tradition stability, operating together.

Perhaps my efforts answered a call made by John Ball many years ago. In an article published in *Folklore* in 1965, Ball points out that every story has the style of the teller as well as the style of his community, and that sometimes a style of the particular tale is distinguishable. He adds, "It would be a very complicated problem to disentangle the social and individual determinants of style, but is a theoretically possible one." [5]

I took this challenge. He was right. It was a complicated problem to try to "disentangle these determinants of style," but it is one that I would undertake again happily. It was a joy to this folklorist's heart to ponder on the art of these storytellers. It is my hope that the readers will enjoy as much as I do these delightful, timelessly appealing stories, and find interesting the results of my efforts to distinguish elements of personal and community style in Del Ringer's and the various community narrators' stories. In the end, one finds the reflection of life in this section of the Salmon River Valley at the turn of the century in these storytelling traditions. Through these tellers' eyes we too can experience life back then. For me, it recaptures that wonder that I knew as a child whenever I heard those fascinating "windy" stories about "the good old days."

You will find the stories have all been transcribed into poetic format, which captures the flavor of each teller's speech.[6] I found that transcribing in this format made it much easier for me to recognize stylistic patterns than prose transcriptions. When I read them I hear in my mind the voices of the tellers. I hope that through the transcriptions and my descriptions of the tellers' art, the readers will be able to share vicariously the experiences these skillful tellers bring to their audiences in a live performance. So, now, as Del Ringer would say, "Dig deep, the guts is on the bottom." It is time for you to meet our master storyteller, Del Ringer.

Chapter One Notes

[1] Toelken, *The Dynamics of Folklore*, 32.

[2] Ong, "Oral Remembering and Narrative Structures," 22.

[3] Edmundson, *Lore*, 199–200. The idea of an individual working with in the bounds of the culture is not unique to Toelken, Ong, and Edmunson, etc. Earlier pioneer folklorist, Stith Thompson notes, "The skillful raconteur usually handles his materials very freely but within traditional limits." *The Folktale* (New York: Dryden Press, 1946), p. 447.

[4] See Labov and Waletzky, "Oral Versions of Personal Experience," 12–44. William Labov and Joshua Waletzky did an important study of the personal experience narrative form. They contend that a personal experience narrative must present an evaluation of its meaning; otherwise it is a mere report, not a true narrative. They argue that the minimum features of a story are a complicating action and an evaluation of the action.

[5] Ball, "Style in the Folktale," 171.

[6] See Tedlock, "On the Translation of Style in Oral Narratives," and Glassie, *Passing the Time in Ballymenone,* for good examples of poetic transcriptions.

Del Ringer, master storyteller
Photo by Ken Auvil, 1972

Chapter Two:
The Life Histories of
Del and Martha Ringer

Del Ringer's roots go deep into the Salmon River country of Idaho. In an interview in October 1985, Martha Harrah Ringer, then his widow, explained:

> You see Del came along just at the right time to hear all these stories from the older people—got 'em clear and was interested in things like that. His grandmother, Hannah Rice, she lived with them and told stories, and he was inquisitive and wanted to hear all those stories. Del would just pick up these stories from the time he was a little tot, about Indians and the local characters, you know, like the Berlinghoff boys. He'd remember those things.

Del's grandmother that Martha spoke of, Hannah Chamberlain Rice, was widowed during the Nez Perce Indian War of 1877. Her husband, Francis, known as Frank, was a blacksmith. Frank was killed not by Indians, but at the hands of a dentist who used dirty pliers to pull an infected tooth, leading to blood poisoning. His widow, Hannah, was a resourceful woman who provided for her family by sewing, cooking for harvest crews, and midwifery. She was left with five young children: Minnie, George, Fred, Nettie, and Gertrude (Del's mother).

Hannah Chamberlain Rice and her brother
Photo courtesy Martha Ringer

I had an opportunity to obtain information from Del's cousin, Mary Auvil. Mary shared with me her mother's (Ruth Eltzroth Hallowell) memoirs about Grandmother Hannah and Mary's mother, who was Hannah's daughter, Nettie. Ruth wrote:

> My mother, Nettie Rice, came from a home made up of women. Her father died during the Nez Perce Indian War when mother was only a few weeks old. She had two brothers but neither was home after she was just a little girl, as they were several years older than my mother. Being without a father, they were thrown into early manhood. So their home consisted of my grandmother, Hannah Rice, and the three girls, Minnie, Nettie, and Gertrude. Grandmother Rice was an immaculate housekeeper, a wonderful cook, and seamstress and well versed in frontier day nursing and midwifery, and a member of the newly

formed Temperance Union. Nettie decided to marry Newt Elzroth and moved in to a bachelor shanty on Davis Bar with him and his brothers and dad. Nettie's sister, Gertrude, was already happily married to Newt's cousin, Will Ringer, Del's father.

According to Martha, the following is written in the handwriting of Nettie Rice Elzroth in the family Bible that Martha Ringer had in her possession and showed to me:

> A story told by Del Ringer gives George the credit for helping with the food supply for the family. He said George dug a well about fourteen feet deep and whenever he found a prairie bird he would throw it into this well, and it would be there when the family needed meat for a meal.

I read in other notes in the family Bible that Del's Uncle George was killed by an acquaintance in a tragic gunfight at Salmon Meadows near Riggins. By the time the family learned of the death, it was too late to attend his funeral. Also noted in the Bible was this remark: "Hannah was noted as a good cook known for her good coffee which she made from grinding barley."

Del himself had told me a lot about his family background as well in our conversation in September of 1975. He said that in 1869, his mother, Gertrude (Gerty) Rice, married William Ringer who was from Missouri. They lived on a farm between Walcox and Almoto, Washington. Del was born in Colfax on July 3, 1897. He was an only child, and remarked, "I guess they decided when I was born, I was ornery enough they didn't want any more."

The family moved to Clarkston in 1902. Will Ringer and Del's uncle (his mother's brother), Fred Rice, both homesteaded there. Martha said that Del acquired his love of the outdoors on his father's ranch there in the Palouse country. Said Del, in September 1975, "We were there with him in the summertime, Mother and I, and I went to Clarkston School in the wintertime."

Del's father, Will, had a good team of horses that he used for hauling in road and building construction. This activity was a family affair. Del related that his mother's brother, Uncle Fred Rice, and his Aunt Nettie's husband, Newt Elzroth, worked with his dad. Del described their work in Lewiston:

> They raised the Fifth Street cut, if you ever been there in Lewiston where it comes down off the hill. Dad had the team and plough, and they had no modern equipment. Ruth's dad drove one team. My mother's brother drove the other. When he'd get stuck on a rock or something he'd just shake it loose. We had the contract in the basin. Dad worked there probably two years. When we left there Dad went out on the Grand River. Then we left the Grand and came back to Lewiston for four or five years before we went up on the Salmon.

Lewiston Hill sign
Photo MHB 1985

In the family Bible, I read that while Will Ringer and Uncle Fred Rice had homesteaded earlier near Waiha, "neither of them proved up so they moved to Slate Creek, Idaho, in 1912." Will Ringer had a homestead there above the Will Chamberlain place.[1] Will Ringer took a job as foreman on Frank Wyatt's ranch near White Bird where Wyatt ran between three and five thousand head of cattle. As a teenager, Del worked on Wyatt's ranch. According to Martha, "Wyatt's ranch was across from where my folks lived. Del worked there as a kid."

Will and Gerty Ringer lived near Slate Creek in a boarding house for stockmen who rented cattle lands. Martha said it was a stop for the old stage and that Del's mom could whip up a meal on short notice when it stopped there. A local schoolteacher boarded with them and Del's grandmother, Hannah.

Old stage stop, White Bird
Photo Grangeville Bicentennial Museum

Martha said:

> His folks moved up where we lived when he was about fifteen, and he lived there until the time we was married. His mother and of course Del's grandmother, because she lived with them, knew all these Indian stories. His grandmother was in it (the Indian War).

> He was always teasing Alice Mahurin. I think one of the things that used to get her was he'd sit behind her and pull her pigtails. Del was funny that way and anyone he liked he'd tease and torment. If it was any one he

didn't particularly care about why he'd just didn't pay attention. A lot of people didn't understand his teasing. It meant he liked 'em.

Del Ringer as a young boy
Photo courtesy Martha Ringer

My sisters went to school with him too. My sister, Alice Harrah, was the same age. He'd boss her for a while, and then she could boss him. She said, "I told him I'd be boss until July; then he could boss rest of the year."

No, he was always teasing, and he loved children. He'd tease them and play with them. He always loved children. In fact before we were married and moved to Spokane, there was a little boy that tagged behind Del everywhere he went. He made promises, and dreams. They were going to homestead together, and work together.

Del quit school at an early age. His folks tried to get him to go back to school but, of course, he didn't want to leave his dad alone up there in the hills doing all the work. They had cattle and rented grazing land. He and his dad were very close, and in business together. I remember Del's comments about how the weather affected their work and lives:

> Ordinarily there, you know, if you didn't get the plowing done in the fall you could plow all winter. There wouldn't be enough frost on the ground to bother. Dad and I plowed forty acres there one winter. Started plowing in January, and had it seeded in February. By gosh, then we went to Lewiston, was gone two weeks, come back, and that damn wheat was about that high.

> There was only the winter of 1919, the only one I seen that was a real rough winter. It got in White Bird (they had a thermometer there) to twenty-two below zero. It didn't vary but a half degree day or night for two weeks. It was really rough.

> Got hot in the summer. God you know, it'd get around 100 or 105. I knew an outfit, surveying the highway up there, North and South. Said the only way they could sleep was lay pillows on the bank and go down and slide in the creek, and that's the way they slept.

Martha said her folks, Wilber and Katherine Harrah, lived on a ridge about five miles from where Del's family settled. Martha was one of twelve children.[2] Her father located their home where, "there was a lovely spring and all the water we needed," said Martha. "It was a log lean-to, and then finally he raised the roof and added an upstairs." Her mother was from Oregon and her father from Indiana. They met in Oregon. After their marriage and the birth of their first three children, they moved to Idaho by covered wagon. Martha's oldest sister, Elbra (ninety-seven years old in 1985 when I recorded her), still remembered that trip. They settled up on the ridge but traveled to the little community of Slate Creek to pick up mail and buy groceries. It was a stop on the old zigzag stage road. Wilber brought the first flock of sheep to the area, causing some animosity among the local cattle ranchers. Eventually, they were accepted into the community as there proved to be enough range for all. Wilber also mined gold at a claim across the river that he reached by boat. When it proved nonproductive, he concentrated on running the ranch up in the hills.

Harrah family homestead, circa 1890
Photo courtesy Martha Ringer

Alice Mahurin recalled, "My Grandmother Large always told about walking up the ridge to see Mrs. Harrah, and I suppose she walked down to see Grandma. They were pioneer people you know." Mrs. Harrah served as midwife for many in the valley. "I remember my mother always being called to come whenever a baby was on the way," said Martha Ringer. Martha added that Mrs. Large came to help her mother, Katherine Harrah, when it was Katherine's time to birth one of her twelve children. She added:

We were a big family. Dad helped mom a lot with the kids. He'd fix breakfast while she'd get the kids dressed. The big boys helped too. We didn't have much but we appreciated what we had. I remember my Dad popping popcorn for us of an evening by the fire. We were poor but we had plenty to eat. I remember we always had a big garden. We raised beef, and Mother dried beans and corn and prunes from the prune tree, canned in gallon jugs.

In those days everybody knew everybody. One thing, in that country you knew everybody for miles, and when somebody come by, they were welcome. Nobody ever went hungry. That was one thing that was important to my mother. I remember one Christmas when two young guys went down to White Bird, and had too much to drink. They drowned trying to swim their horses across the river. I was just a little kid, but I remember Mom saying she hoped they had a good last meal. There was no such thing as a stranger. It was a hard life but a good life.

Martha said she remembered when she first met her future husband, Del Ringer, when she was a little girl. She went down to White Bird to visit her oldest sister Elbra, and to play with Dr. Foskett's little girl. Del stopped by Elbra's and asked Elbra, "Who is your little friend?" As Del and Martha grew up, they got to know each other better and enjoyed seeing each other at the community dances at the schoolhouse, and on occasions like the Fourth of July picnic.

Martha Harrah at age eighteen
Photo courtesy Martha Harrah Ringer

Martha's mother died in 1918. Martha said, "My father just couldn't bear to stay up on the ridge without her." Wilber Harrah moved the family to Spokane, where they had been preceded by two of the older girls. Wilber worked there as a fireman. Alice Harrah took care of the home, and the older girls worked in the local sanitarium.

Wilbur and Alice Harrah in Spokane
Photo courtesy Martha Ringer

Del followed Martha, and they were married on June 7, 1920. They had a simple double ceremony with her sister, Alice, and Grover Hearing. Grover had been one of the boarders the Harrahs took in their home to help with expenses. Martha gave me a photo of the two couples on their twenty-fifth anniversary. Del told me, "Martha made me walk the plank when we got married." I didn't understand his remark until his grandson, John Day, later explained to me:

"She made me walk the plank. That's the God's truth." Gramps maintained that, and maintained that, and by gosh it was true. The four of them was married up at Newport, and the church was being remodeled, and they were digging around the foundation, and they had an old plank going up to the door. Alice Haring, her sister, was married the same day, and the four of them celebrated their anniversary together. Granny's got a big article on it. [3] Del tried the life of a city dude for a short while in Spokane, working for the Armour packing plant, but he just wasn't cut out for that kind of life. He soon decided, "I'm going back to Idaho where I don't have to make a pack horse out of myself. We have horses and mules to do it."

Del and his bride moved back to join his parents, Will and Gerty Ringer, on the homestead on Slate Creek. During those early years, they often spent time together fishing for recreation. Martha said, "I just loved to fish. After I finished working in the house, I'd put on overalls, and go out and help 'em haying in the fields, so we could hurry up and go fishing." According to Martha, all one had to do was put a grasshopper on the line, and every cast of the old willow pole into the Salmon would land a nice trout. One could get as many as they wanted, though the limit was supposedly about twenty pounds. It was not unusual to catch up to a hundred fish in a day. They would cook them up on the spot with a little salt and grease in an old fry pan for a picnic with perhaps some bread, and take the rest home for family and friends.

They also enjoyed Saturday night dances at the schoolhouse, and at the dance hall in White Bird that doubled as a movie theater twice a week. Del said there was a flume out of White Bird Creek that came down to a water wheel that generated electricity for the movie. When the flume got full of sucker fish, the lights would go out and the film would be lost until somebody would dig the suckers out of the waterwheel and they could start the show again. Del described it as follows:

> They'd have the picture show in back of the old Coomb Building. Generally about the middle of the picture show, by gosh, old Ben Davis would jump up when the lights would commence to flicker and go see. He'd have to dig the suckers out. Then the lights would come on again and somebody'd say, "Ben's got the suckers."

Old White Bird flume
Photo courtesy Grangeville Bicentennial Museum

I got the impression Del liked to play practical jokes in those years. It seems a ditch full of suckers used to run through Ed Smith's livery stable in White Bird. Del said that one night he and his buddies pitchforked up one of the fish and put it in a high window of the office of the little White Bird newspaper, *The Salmon Sun*. "That darn old sucker lay there and rotted," said Del. It seems the editor had taken the part of someone not well liked locally. Del said the editor wrote, it was "the darnest smell he'd ever smelled and offered fifty dollar reward for whoever done it." The reward was never collected as "nobody was going to squeal." Maybe I can collect it since I am spilling the goods on him after all these years.

Smith's livery barn, White Bird
Photo courtesy Grangeville Bicentennial Museum

Those were very happy years along the Salmon for Will and Gerty Ringer, and Del and his young bride, until about 1928 when there was a bad slump in the farming business. The family sold what they had and moved to Buena, Washington, near Yakima, where they lived working in the fruit industry before coming to North Bend, Washington, in 1936. They had cousins in Buena who had come ahead of them. These were Newt and Nettie Elzroth. Their daughter, Ruth Elzroth, who like Del was an only child, was like a sister to Del as they had grown up together when the families worked together in Lewiston. Mr. Elzroth had been a bookkeeper in a packinghouse for some time. Another brother worked as a foreman on a fruit ranch. Encouraged by these connections, the entire family, including Del and Martha's daughter, Norma, and Grandmother Hanna, moved to Buena in 1928. Will, Gerty, Del, and Martha worked in the fruit packing houses. Del also clerked in a grocery store.

The Ringers and the Elzroths lived as a close family in those years, often telling stories of the old days along the Salmon. Martha said:

> Del's cousin Ruth's folks, the Elzroths, and Del's dad were double cousins, as they had married sisters, and were just like brothers, raised together and all. We would

get together on an evening and tell these stories, and talk and things like that. We just lived in a circle there in Buena and we'd get together for potluck dinners. We'd have fun, talk, and enjoy being together.

Will Ringer and Grandmother Hannah Rice died and are buried in Buena. Gerty Ringer went with her son Del, Martha, and granddaughter Norma, when they moved to North Bend in 1936. They were unhappy with the uncertain nature of the work in Buena, and had heard there were good jobs with Weyerhaeuser in North Bend. Del hired on, learned quickly, and worked with various foremen. Before long he was hired as a millwright, a position he held for twenty-six years. Soon Martha's sister Alice, and husband, Grover Hearing, also moved to North Bend, where Grover found work in the lumber mill, too. Upon retirement, Del stayed in North Bend, occasionally enjoying some time fishing with his cousin Ruth's family on outings to Lake Patterson and to property on Whidbey Island they had purchased together. These outings ended when Del suffered a stroke after which reminiscing about the old days became an even more important activity for him.

During his active years in North Bend, Del's family had a small farm on Highland Drive. There, Martha related, Del continued to find an audience for his tales of the Salmon River. It seems Del was a regular pied piper. Martha recalled one relationship with a sister's son:

> I don't remember which one, but when we used to live over on Highland Drive, this boy was about twelve or fourteen years old. Del would go to work in the late afternoon. This boy used to come home from school and get his chores done just as fast as he could so he could come over and listen to Del's stories.

Their daughter Norma's children also spent a great deal of time with their grandparents, particularly during the war when Norma's husband was in the service. One of Del's grandsons, John Day, now a chiropractor in Spokane, told his grandmother, "Nobody will ever know how much that man meant to me." As a boy he had trailed in his grandfather's footsteps like a shadow. Martha relates that a neighbor once said to her, "My husband gets the biggest kick out of the way that boy's at his feet all the time, just talking away." Martha says that when John returned to Spokane, his other grandfather would say, "You can always tell when John's been at the Ringers. He acts just like Del." That remark made me eager to meet John and sure enough when I interviewed him in 1986, I found he was a storyteller just like his grandfather.

Obviously family relationships were important to the Ringers. John cherished his relationship with his grandfather, saying:

> He really gave us a heritage. He'd take us on trips when we was kids, like over to Spokane, and in the car he'd sing songs like, "Monkey he got drunk, and sat on the elephants trunk," " It ain't going to rain no more no more," and then he'd sing "doodle-daddle, doddle-daddle, doot, dat, doot." He and I was always going to have a ranch together. When you come down US 90 toward Vantage, as you start up the hill there, there is that big canyon that ran back a ways. "We'll put the barn in here," he'd say, "and the corral over there." Then he'd really get into it, and start on the old stories about the old days along the Salmon.[3]

Del's cousin, Ruth Elzroth Hallowell, and her daughter, Mary Hallowell Auvil, were among his greatest fans. Mary wrote to me in a letter dated September 10, 1982, about their fishing trips and family get-togethers. She tape recorded her "uncle" on one of these outings in the sixties. While his stories have been known primarily to his family, they are a rich treasure that Mary and the others have graciously agreed to share with me and with a wider audience. She wrote:

> When was I first attracted to Uncle Del's stories? They are part of the family lore. The Ringers lived next door to my grandparents in Buena, Washington. When he and Aunt Martha moved to Seattle area, my brother and I spent many spring vacations with Uncle Del and Aunt Mart, and I suppose that is when we first paid

attention to his stories. I guess the most gratifying result I experienced from recording his stories and then transcribing them was a letter I received from the Ringers' first grandchild, Diana Day, who has been deaf since she was two when she had spinal meningitis. She wrote to me that she enjoyed reading the stories. She knew that her grandfather always storied about his past but didn't know what he said. Now she could read it.

My acquaintance with the Ringers took place in their retirement years in their home in North Bend, evidently the scene of many good conversations. Martha said:

Del loved to talk. He liked to talk to people. When we'd have a group come in, I was always thankful for him. He would entertain them with his stories and I enjoyed him. He never knew a stranger.

Del died on April 12, 1984. It is a rare privilege to have known him and to have heard his stories. He may be gone, but his legacy lives on in the memories of his family, and in stories of the Salmon River pioneers.

Chapter Two Notes

[1] See Chesdsey and Frei, *Idaho County Voices,* 201, for a mention of Will and Gertrude Ringer as living near Slate Creek in 1914, when Grandmother Hannah Rice's brother, William Chamberlain, came to visit them and decided to settle there as well.

[2] In May 1996, Martha shared with me a letter Katherine Warfield Harrah wrote to her mother. The letter was dated Freedom, Idaho, December 28, 1904. In it Katherine wrote eleven of the Harrah children's names, their birthdates, and "the names I call them":

Elbra Caroline,	born April 17, 1888,	Elbra
James Marvin,	born March 14, 1889,	Marvin
Julious Virgil,	born August 19, 1891,	Virgil
Lloyd Wilber,	born March 7, 1893,	Lloyd
Mary Violet,	born August 14, 1894,	Violet
Nannie Gladys,	born December 1, 1895,	Gladys
Alice Margret,	born December 1, 1895,	Alice
Floyd Raymond,	born September 15, 1898,	Raymond
Maud Elmira,	born April 19, 1900,	Maud
Martha Anna Della,	born March 31, 1902,	Martha
Katherine Gertrude,	born September 3, 1904,	Gertrude

The last Harrah daughter, Georgia, was born later, November 1, 1910. Georgia was just eight years old when Katherine died in November 3, 1918. Wilber Harrah died October 26, 1926.

[3] The quotes from John Day in this chapter come from an interview which took place at the Westin Hotel, Seattle, February 8, 1986.

Chapter Three:
Old Man Wyatt and his Hands

The Berlinghoff boys lived not far from Old Man Wyatt. He said they was good hands, but just as simple as could be. They played the fiddle, but could only play one tune, "The Fisherman's Hornpipe." Old George Bean was pretty disgusted the way they carried on up at dances. Old Ed called up the Berlinghoffs. Said "George would like to hear you boys play 'The Fisherman's Hornpipe'." Damned if the boys didn't call up Old George and play it for him on the phone. He was asleep in bed. He was ready to kill whoever done it.

—Del Ringer, 1982

Del Ringer told a number of different types of stories. Many were his own personal experience narratives. Some were supposedly true third person stories about others. His favorite type was the local character anecdote, a single incident told in the third person as truth that emphasizes unusual personality traits of its subject. He also told a few local history stories about events that were well-known community-wide. From his teen years when he worked on Frank Wyatt's ranch comes a group of stories about "Old Man Wyatt" and his hands.

Frank Wyatt was known in his day as the "Cattle King of Idaho." In 1883, he came to White Bird, Idaho, from Colorado, and established his Bow and Arrow Ranch near Deer Creek. He employed many cowboys on his extensive ranch which extended from the Salmon River to the Snake River, and as far north as the forks of the two rivers, even including an area in Oregon.[1] Del always called him "Old Man Wyatt." It seems that Del always referred to his characters as "old," no matter what their age.

Frank "Old Man" Wyatt
Courtesy Cort Conley

Among Del's family's favorite stories were the ones he told about a couple of Old Man Wyatt's hands, the Berlinghoff Brothers, Jake and Frank Berlinghoff. Martha would say to Del, "Tell her the before and behind story, you know, the Hayracks." Del told it in all of the five storytelling sessions from which I made transcriptions from 1973 to 1982, as well as in a recording his niece made of his stories in the 1960s. I have spaced the transcriptions to suggest the phrasing that Del used.

"The Hayracks"[2]
Del Ringer, 1973

Well, Old Man Wyatt hired the Berlinghoffs to help in haying.
They wanted to know how to make the hayracks.
He told 'em,
    "Just make a flat bed on the hay wagon,
        and make a tailgate."
(Not to put any side boards on 'em or anything.)

So they made 'em.
Well, they couldn't figure out
    how they was going to tell which was which.
And they made 'em.

And there was stirrups went on the wagon,
    on the cross feet in front and behind.

    "You just pick 'em up and set 'em down
        in them damn stirrups."

They couldn't tell how they was going to tell
    the Before from the Behind.
Finally Jake, he come up with a bright idea.

    "We'll just put B for Before, Frank."

    "Yeah, Jake, and we'll put B for Behind."

So they laid 'em out by the wagons.
There was five of them damn wagons,
    and old man sent over the next morning.
He said,
    "Go put the tailgates on boys.
    We'll be over."
He was going to have 'em pitch in the field.

They went over to the teams,
    and the old man he was over in the field.

They didn't come, and they didn't come.
Finally the guys with the teams
    was getting such a kick out of it.

They were so darned tickled at them trying
    to figure out which end was which.

The night before Clay Davis and I passed the old barn
    where they'd built the hay wagons.
And by gosh, we'd seen what they'd done.
So we took and piled 'em all up together, you see.
And by gosh, they was all piled up together.
And they couldn't tell the Befores from the Behinds.

The old man he went over and said,
    "What's the matter with you guys?
    Why aren't you getting over there and getting 'em on
        and let the boys bring the wagons over?"

"Well," they said,
"We had 'em laid out and we marked 'em
    B for Before and B for Behind.
We had 'em laying front and back of the wagons.
Somebody come along in the night
    last night and piled 'em all in one pile.
Now we can't tell the Before from the Behind."

Old man says,
    "You damn crazy bitches,
    you didn't have to mark them.
All you had to do was to set them
    up there on them stirrups.
They are all made the same."

They couldn't figure that out.
The boys with the teams
    they was just came near dying.
Had to laugh at 'em
    thinking how funny it was.

They weren't the brightest boys.

Them stirrups were just the same.
And the cross piece in front and back
    were just the same.
They were set the same distance.

Haying in Salmon River country
Photo courtesy Grangeville Bicentennial Museum

Clay and Emma Davis in 1943.

Clay and Emma Davis
Photo courtesy Cort Conley

Evidently the Berlinghoffs had a long-standing reputation in the community as colorful characters. In 1985 when I made my first trip to the Salmon River country, I asked Archie Hadorn, an old-timer who had driven the stage when he was young, if he knew the Berlinghoffs. He replied, "Yep, they was sure characters alright, but I ain't seen Frank since 1914." (Frank was killed in World War I in France.) Del Ringer told Mary Auvil in 1965 that after the war there was a dance in White Bird for the returning boys who had served. Del said Jake was running around grabbing everyone to shake hands and saying, "By the Gods, the sons-of-britches got one of us. They killed old Frank!"

Archie Hadorn, incidentally, provided a lively description of the dances he attended in this youth. Archie said after all day on the cattle drive, he'd ride into town for the dance, dance all night, and then ride back out to the job in the morning with no sleep. "Boy, it was tough," he said. When I visited the area again in 1994, I found that Archie Hadorn had passed on. His gravestone marks his World War I service.

Archie Hadorn's grave
Photo MHB 1994

When I asked Del if he had any more stories about the Berlinghoffs, that first day I met him, Del told the story of the "Dance with the Berlinghoffs." He told this story on all five of our recording occasions, from 1973 to 1982, so evidently it was one of the standard stories in his repertoire. It appears that not only did the Berlinghoffs bungle on the job for Wyatt, they didn't do much better on the social front either.

"Dance with the Berlinghoffs"[3]
Del Ringer, 1973

The Berlinghoff boys.

There was a dance across the river on Saturday night,
    and the Beans went.
Guy, the Brother and there was two girls.

Guy, and the little fellow,
(His name was Ray.)
Guy, he was about my age,
    and one of the girls and I
    used to be pretty good friends.

Annie, the oldest girl, was kind of a sympathetic girl.
Over at Seth Jones' one night they had a dance.
She kind of took pity on Jake and Frank.
They were setting back in the corner.
Go and ask some girl to dance
    and they'd make an excuse.

Annie told two girls that was cousins of hers,
    and turned 'em down and make excuses,

    "You girls are ornery."

They said,
    "Well, bet you wouldn't dance with 'em."

    "You just wait and see!"

So pretty soon, one of 'em went and asked Annie.
She got out, and danced with him.
She hadn't more than finished the dance
    'til the next one went.
So she danced with him.

God! They just about like to
    run her to *death* that night.

So Guy and I told 'em,
    "Kind of think Annie's got a case on you guys.
    You better come over tomorrow and see her."
We didn't think anything about it.

It was eight miles from their place to town.
It was spring and the roads was bad.
It was breaking up.
And I was going from downtown home.

Went by Beans, and by gosh!
There on the front porch was the two Berlinghoffs,
    and Annie standing by the door waiting for 'em.

They had on a pair of old muddy bib overalls.
There was mud on them overalls,
    prettinear to their knees,
And overshoes, them dirty, dirty overshoes, and
    them muddy overalls was on the front porch.
So they went, and got 'em off, and went into the house.

I waved at Annie when I went by.
and she looked over that way,
    and looked foolish as the dickens.

Next morning I got a hold of Guy and said,
    "Don't you think we ought take the Berlinghoffs
        to Sunday School and Church?"
And Guy said,
    "Yeah, a good idea."
So they went with us.
They was a-lookin' at the hymn book,
    and I don't remember what hymn was
        the preacher asked to be sung.

But anyhow,
    the chorus the second time around as omitted.
It was wrote there, "*omit.*"

They wanted to know,
    "What's that word?"
and we told 'em.

Guy was setting on one side of 'em,
    and I was setting on the other.
We kept digging 'em in the ribs, saying,
    "*sing, sing.*"

Whispered to 'em,
    "Sing louder."

They just sounded like a couple of bulls a-bellerin'.

They come to the part
    where the chorus was to be omitted.
They sang,
    "*and omit!*"

The preacher was so damn tickled he had to laugh.

Annie said,
    "You dirty devils,
    if ever you do me trick like that again,
    I'm going to have a brother and friend of his
that's *among the missing!*"

But they stayed all day
    and stayed until it was getting dark,
        before they started back home,
And they'd walked that eight miles over to White Bird.

They was *characters all right*!

In a couple of the versions Del included an exaggerated description
of how it was to dance with the wallflower, Hattie:

Boy, they'd play that waltz
it seem like for an hour.
Boy, if you danced with Hattie
you didn't have much skin
from your knees to your ankles.

Odd Fellow Hall, scene of White Bird dances
Photo MHB 1995

Downtown White Bird
Photo MHB 1995

In 1979, I asked Del, "What's your favorite memory of those guys?" He answered by singing, "I'm Jacob Berlinghoff. Don't you know me?" Then he followed with an interesting little introduction to the story that was included in a 1965 version that his cousin Mary Auvil sent me. It was a comic opening in which the Berlinghoffs introduced themselves.

He did not repeat it in later tellings to me, but I suspect that if one could have eavesdropped on all the tellings in his lifetime, one would find this to be a frequently repeated segment. Imagine if you will him telling this story as Del imitated the Berlinghoffs' dull and ignorant voices:

"The Berlinghoff Boys"
Del Ringer, 1979

All you had to do was get a couple of us ornery cusses around,
    "Go on, Go on,
        there's a girl over there.
    God dang,
        she's just a-dyin' to dance with you."
Get 'em started, see.
They'd go.
They didn't give a damn.

Well, the girls decided the way to get rid of them was to say,
    "No, I can't dance with you.
    I don't know you."

And by God, they'd immediately introduce themselves,
    "Why I'm Frank Berlinghoff,
    by the Gods, I'm Frank Berlinghoff."
    "By the Gods, I'm Jacob Berlinghoff."

We'd get the biggest kick out of that.

His audiences always asked for stories about the "boys." Fortunately for his audiences, Del never tired of telling stories about the Berlinghoffs and their ignorance. They certainly weren't up to date with an understanding of things of the modern world like electricity. Del must have liked this story about "The Battery" because he told it at all of our recording occasions. He characterized the Berlinghoffs as loving to talk, even if they didn't seem to know what they were talking about. Del rendered his dialogue with a dull, but innocent, voice for Jake. Del, of course, portrayed himself and his friend, Clay Davis, whom we

met in "The Hayracks," as fully understanding the situation, and once
again having to explain things to a Berlinghoff.

"The Battery"
Del Ringer, 1975

There were two Berlinghoffs,
    Frank and Jake.
We was going to White Bird one morning,
    and we met Jake.
He had something in a gunny sack
    throwed over his shoulder._
They had an old Chevrolet Car.
You'd meet one of them,
    and, my gosh, they'd talk all day!
Well, he kept a- squirmin' around
    while he was talkin'.
We said to him,
    "What's the matter with you Jake?"

    "Well, the battery is dead in my car.
    And I took it over to White Bird to have it changed."
(It was about eight miles to their place.
You had to cross the Salmon by ferryboat.)
Jake, he said,
    "I took it over in the hack."

    "Why didn't you go after in the hack?"

    "Because that old Injun charges twenty-five cents
    to cross in a team, and only ten cents by foot."
(He wasn't going to pay him an extra fifteen cents.
He'd walk back carrying that battery in a gunny sack.)

Jake, he said,
    "You know, the goddamn electricity has run out
        through my overshirt, my undershirt, and on my back!"

Clay turned around and said,
    "Turn around and take it down."

And, my gosh, the acid had leaked out and run out
　　and took the back out of his shirt and undershirt!
Clay said,
　　"You know, you damn simpleton.
　　Don't you know that it is likely to eat you too?"
　　"Well, what is it?
　　It's electricity isn't it?"

Clay said,
　　"No, it's the acid in the battery."
There weren't much left to hold the battery,
　　but he finally got it up on his back.
You'd meet 'em, and they'd stop
　　and talk to you as long as you'd stay and talk to them.

Old car on White Bird Hill
Photo Courtesy Granville Bicentennial Museum

Old ferry across the Salmon River
Photo courtesy Grangeville Bicentennial Museum

"Old Man Wyatt" had another ignorant hand, a son-in-law, about whom Del storied. In 1891 when Frank Wyatt moved from Greeley, Colorado, he brought his wife and three daughters. Mrs. Wyatt, the former Margaret Ellen Conne of Philadelphia, did not care for ranch life, and lived in a home in Lewiston with the girls. They made only summer visits to the ranch. In "The Dude," Del told about a fellow from the east that Wyatt's youngest daughter, Blanche, married, and who worked for his father-in-law for a while.

"The Dude"[4]
Del Ringer, 1973

Old Man Wyatt.
He had a daughter married a fellow from the east.
Her mother wouldn't have anything else.
All the girls had to go east to finishing school.

Two of 'em come back and
    married men up in that country.
The favorite daughter of the old man was the youngest one.

She went east and
   a fellow got powerfully stuck on her.
Followed her to the ranch.
Married her out here.
(The ranch was between the rivers,
   the Snake and the Salmon.)
He was about the most
   ignorant devil you ever saw.
He'd never been out of the city!

The old man was quite a guy to raise a big garden.
Over in the back end of the place he had about five acres.
He was over there working one day.

This fellow Blanche had married was named Harry.
He went over to the old man to see what he was doing.
Wanted to help him.
   "This is the way you can help me the most.
   Thought I had a hoe over here.
   Go over to the tool house and get me a hoe."
He got on his horse and beat it over to the tool house.
He was gone *God knows how long*!

Finally he come back.
Brings him a shovel!
Old man, he says,
   "I didn't tell you to bring me a shovel.
   I told you bring me a hoe!"
He said,
   "I looked around and that was as near a hoe as I figured."

"Well," he said,
   "Get on your horse and come over here with me.
   I'll show you the difference between a shovel and a hoe!"

The old man had some sheep around the ranch.
They watered the stock they had in the barn from the creek.
Harry went down to the creek with Clay Davis.
He'd seen some sheep tracks in the creek.

Harry says,
  "What kind of animal makes that?"
Clay says,
  "That's a sheep track,
  See two toes, the split hoof."

  "What kind of a track is this?"
Clays says,
  "That's a horse track."
He said,
  "Well, what's this over here?"

  "Why that's a cow track.
  It's bigger than a sheep's.
  It's got a split hoof too."

  "What kind of animal makes this?"

(They was turkey tracks.)

  "See, it's got five toes too.
  What kind of animal makes that?"

He was about as *ignorant* as anything can be.

He said himself he was never out of the city but once.
He was born and raised in Philadelphia.
He said,
  "I was never out of the city but once
        and it was only for a few hours."

He went back.
Somebody asked the Old Man,

  "Where is Harry?"
He says,
  "Oh, the old grandmammy died.
  Left him a barrel of ten, twenty dollar gold pieces.
  He went back to get them."

The attitude Del clearly presented in this story was that characters like the Dude offer a source of amusement in their bungling attempts to do the ordinary. Similarly, Ken Auvil, Del's cousin Mary Auvil's husband, who observed Del on many storytelling occasions, remarked in a January 1986 interview:

> The loggers and people in my hometown [Mineral, Washington] look on people who are a little different as comical. They don't really have scorn for them, but they do look on them as a source of amusement. I always had the sense that Uncle Del looked at people that way. He was amused by them, talked about them, and that was his kind of entertainment.

Del himself, of course, was one of Old Man Wyatt's hands. When he personally appeared in the story as a main character he portrayed himself as cool-headed. Here is Del's story about the time he and Wyatt met an angry man with a gun. Del told me that until he moved to North Bend, he always carried a gun. I presume such encounters were not unusual in the early days in the Northwest

"Kanky and the Mules"
Del Ringer, 1973

When I was working for old man Wyatt,
    he had a bunch of little fourteen 'n a half Cayuse Mules.
He had bought up a lot of places.
One had bought from Bob Kanky.

There was a fellow came in there
homesteaded.
Homesteaded there
    and had a family right next to the Kanky place.
The old man figured the fellow was kind of hard up.
Said,
    "You can live on the Kanky place.
    Farm that as well as your own."
So he put in a crop.

Well, one night them darn mules come along,
    and jumped the fence
What they didn't eat up they trampled down
    and raised the dickens.

Old man Wyatt and I was one day out on the plains.
    "Let's go over by the Kanky place,
            and see how that old guy is doin'."

We went over there.
The old guy saw us come.
And he thought some outfit had come
    the night before and tore his fences down,
            and turned them mules in there.

By gosh,
He come meeting us with a thirty/thirty.
He had it all cocked, and
By gosh, there was a hole in the barrel,
    looked *big* enough to crawl into!
He had it cocked and was jumping around laughin'.

The old man said,
    "Kid, let's just keep a-ridin', right through.
    If we turn and start away from him,
    he's goin' to shoot us."

By gosh, we kept a-ridin'.
    Pulled up.
The old man wasn't too badly scared,
    and I wasn't as scared as I thought I was.

The old man was riding
    a big old bay horse he used to ride.
The guy kept coming to us
    jumping all around, and cussing.
Had the barrel of the gun right in the old man's face.

Old man said,
"You better be careful.
That thing is liable to go off and hurt somebody."

Old man said,
"We never did nothing.
Them mules jumped the fence;
Can you show us anyplace the fence is tored down?"

"Nope," he couldn't.

Them mules wasn't in there the next morning.
They had jumped back out
by the time we got down talking to the old guy.

Old Man Wyatt, he said,
"You come into this country.
I figured I was doing you a favor
letting you live on this place.
I see I made an awful mistake."

The old fellow felt terrible.
He started a-cryin' just like a kid,

"I was mistaken
I suppose I'll have to move out."

"No, you don't have to move out.
Just be a little more sure about things."

As we turned to go I said to him,

"God, the hole in that barrel of the gun was
big enough to crawl in!
Were you scared?"

"Hell, yes I was scared,
but wasn't no use to let him know."

Del Ringer really relished telling tales about the old days on Old Man Wyatt's Bow and Arrow Ranch. We can conclude that in those days on the ranch there was respect for hands who knew how to do the jobs and conduct themselves as brave men, but there was ridicule for those who bungled and acted foolishly on the job or off.

Chapter Three Notes

[1] For a description of Frank Wyatt's ranch see Chedsey and Frei's *Idaho County Voices*, 298–99.

[2] "The Hayracks" is related to Motif J 1922, "Marking the Place" and also to J 2700, "The easy problem made hard." Motifs may be located in Thompson, *Motif Index of Folk Literature*.

[3] "Dance with the Berlinghoffs" is related to K 1210, "Humiliated or ruffled lovers," and also to K 1006, "Dupe induced to incriminate himself: taught incriminating song or persuaded to wear incriminating clothes."

[4] "The Dude" could be classified under J 1711, "The city person ignorant of the farm."

Chapter Four:
The Jewetts

Local characters? That country was full of them. Why
Old Jewett lived right next to us. Old Jewett's ranch
joined Dad's. One time the girls ganged up on him at a
dance. It was Ruth, Alma, May, Dolly, and Norma. They
called a lady's choice. I got the first one of them to tag
Bill. One was a dancin', then another; danced Old Bill
to death. He couldn't dance, just jump up and down.
Ruth and Alma said they didn't have any skin from their
knees to their ankles. Them big feet of his skinned 'em
up. Boy, he thought he was having a real time.

—Del Ringer, 1973

There were other local characters beside the Berlinghoffs whom Del
portrayed as simpletons in his stories. Everyone always begged Del
to tell stories about the Jewetts. Old Preston Jewett, Old Lady Rose
Jewett, and their son, Old Bill, appeared as characters in many of
Del's tales. Incidentally, Del was well into telling local character stories
about the Jewetts long before his niece Mary Auvil first recorded him
in 1965. There is evidence he was at it even back in the 1940s. In our
conversation in January 1986, Mary Auvil said:

I remember when we went to Seattle in the early 1940s,
and Uncle Del and Aunt Mart were in North Bend

then. My dad, and Uncle Frank, and Del talked about the old days. We kids would hear 'em and say, "Now they're on Old Buena, or Old Frank, or Old Bill Jewett." They would tell about all those old characters.

Here is the version of "Jewett's Saddle" that Mary Auvil recorded:

"Jewett's Saddle"[1]
Del Ringer, 1965

Old Bill brought a new saddle.
Christ,
    in the wintertime
he was riding that damn mule of his
    and he was riding it *bareback*.

    "How come Bill?
    What have you done with your saddle?"

Bill, he said,
    "I'm not going to put that new saddle
        on that damn mule,
    and have it go
    ass over teakettle down the hill
    and skin my saddle up!"

If the mule went
    ass over teakettle
        down the hill
    that was alright,
    Bill, would slide off it,

But,
he wasn't going to put his new saddle on it,
    and have his saddle
    all skinned up
        with that mule going

    Ass over teakettle!

Del Ringer told another great story about Bill Jewett and his dad, Old Jewett, in which they tried to turn off the old lady's nagging about a leaking roof by a bungled attempt to fix it.

"Jewett's Roof"[2]
Del Ringer, 1965

Bill Jewett couldn't make the mental test.

Old Jewett was explaining
why Bill was turned down,
and Old Roy Gordon was there,
and Old Jewett said,

> "The damn doc hit Bill on the knee
> with the rubber hammer,
> and because his leg didn't jerk
> *they turned him down!*"

Old Roy said:
"Damn it Jewett,
are you sure you got that right?
Are you sure they didn't
hit him on the *head* with the hammer?"

By God, but you take them two outfits.
Old Jewett and Bill,
went up by there one time
They had an old log house.

There was an attic.
I guess the kids all slept up in the attic,
because the main part of it was just one room,
and that was the living room,
and his and the old lady's

Then he had built an—
Oh—about twelve-by-twelve shed on the side of it.
And he put one by twelves on the roof
and battened the cracks.

Well, of course then that damn lumber dried out,
you know,
  and kind of got old and cured.

Why, the battens curled up, and
why the water run in, and the old lady,
    she'd raise the devil about it.

What could he do, but go out
    and take the boys, and some shovels,
    and he'd throw dirt up on top of it,
you know.

Of course, the rain would wash the dirt down,
    and kind of plug it up for a little while.
Then the dry weather would come,
    and here come a rain again,
    and the damn dirt would wash right out.

    "So my God,"
he said,
    "the old lady kept raising Hell,
    and the kitchen a-leakin'."
    "So the other day,"
He said,
    "I was down to White Bird, and
    that goddamn Nevins sold me some
    of that new fangled roofing paper."
Old Jewett said,
    "Tar paper stuff, only a lot heavier."
    (It was roll roofing.)
    "He sold me that, and I brought it home."
    "Boy, I'll have the roof fixed for the old lady."
He said,
    "I told Bill to put it on."

He got up on the roof
    and put it on like they said.
Nailed it down like they said,
and he said,
    "First time it rained,
    by God,"
he said,
    "it leaked worse than it ever did before!"

This will show you how smart he is.

Instead of running the paper in
    under the eaves of the shake roof,
he just took her up on the roof
    and nailed her down, see.

Well, Jesus,
that just made a trough
    for all that water to run in under the paper.

Then,
he had the paper nailed down pretty good
    down on the lower end,
you know,
    and it wouldn't run off the shed,
    and it backed up,
    and like to drown the old lady.

Old Jewett,
he cussed Nevins
    black and blue for selling him something.

You know,
    he wasn't much brighter than Old Bill,
you know when you stop to think about it.

There was sure some real characters
    in that country.

Old store along Route 95
Photo MHB 1995

Evidently Old Jewettt was not only considered simple, but rather stubborn as well. I heard Del tell a story of Old Jewett's death on only two occasions, but Del was consistent in the details of the story in both of them.

Dr. Wilson Foskett, who attended Old Jewett, was a dedicated country doctor who made his rounds on horseback, practicing medicine and surgery under primitive conditions.[3] Dr. Foskett was killed in an accident in 1924 when his car plunged into the Salmon while he was making a night call.

"Rattlesnake Kills Old Jewett"
Del Ringer 1982

At Slate Creek
there was a blackberry patch.
Jewett and the Old lady was down there
    picking blackberries, and
the rattlesnakes was pretty bad.
They was a-picking and,
    Old Jewettt,
the rattlesnake bit him.

He said,
 "Just a thorn."
Was in his finger, and
 he was a-suckin away at the thorn
  with his mouth.

I don't think he had a good tooth
 in his head.

The old lady said,
 "That sounded to me
  like a rattlesnake."

He said,
 "It was just a damn thorn.
 I was reaching down underneath
  the blackberries,
  and I got a thorn in my finger."

They called the doctor,
  Dr. Foskett at White Bird.

The old man lived about a week
  after he got snakebit.

She got him to go in and lay down,
  and she went back up there
  and hunted around
  and found the rattlesnake
  and killed it.

Then she came back,
  and told the old man about it.
He said,
 "No, it was just a damn thorn."

By then,
 she could see the place where the fangs went in.

"Well, I guess you got two thorns
          then didn't you!"

Old Doc Foskett,
he come up.
He said,
     if he could have been there
               right at the time, why
     he could have done something for him.

His head was swelled.
You couldn't even tell he was
               a human being.

Doc said,
     his tongue was swelled up so bad,
     it stuck out of his mouthd,

"It was the worse looking sight
          I ever seen."

Old man was stubborn right to the end.
     He still wouldn't give up.

Dr. Wilson Foskett on his horse
Photo courtesy Grangeville Bicentennial Museum

Like the stories about the Berlinghoffs, these stories about the Jewetts exhibited Del Ringer's consistent storytelling skills. All Del had to do was mention "Jewett," and listeners smiled and prepared themselves to listen to an engaging local character anecdote.

Chapter Four Notes

[1] "Jewett's Saddle" is related to J 2500, "Foolish extremes."

[2] "Jewett's Roof" could be indexed J 2171.2, "Short sightedness in roofing."

[3] Chedsey and Frei, *Idaho County Voices,* 305.

Chapter Five:
Wild Creature Stories

That old guy kept sucking on that place where a "hornet" stung him. Suck his mouth full of the stuff. That old man had so much of that poison in his system, his tongue, his tongue was hanging out his mouth. Darnest thing I ever saw.

—Del Ringer, 1982

In addition to storying about rattlesnakes and insect bites, it should be no surprise that Del Ringer participated in what appeared to be a valley storytelling tradition of recounting tales of encounters with wild creatures such as cougars, bears, coyotes, elk, and deer. These animals were prevalent in the country where he spent his youth. Storying about these encounters appears to have been a good pastime in the Salmon River country for a long time. Usually his stories were full of bravado, but Del admitted that as a boy he felt some fear when he met a cougar.

"The Cougar Scare"
Del Ringer 1979

When I was about sixteen,
    there was a cougar.
We could hear him.

There was twenty acres of pasture
    where we kept the milk cows.
My gosh,
we went out to get the cows one night,
    and the cows was gone.
I knew they was probably over
        in the other forty acre pasture in the back.
I knew there was timber in there.

This cougar had killed a packhorse.
We found him a couple of days before.

I got to the other pasture
    and closed the gate,
    and that cougar let out a yell.
Sounded like he was
    right on the other side of the fence.

What scared me was
    the horse started to run.
I had hold of the bridle ring.

My gosh,
I don't think she had much more than turned,
    and started to run,
        until I landed on her back.

Boy,
I got to whipping her on both sides.

Got to the barn,
    opened the barn door,
    pulled off the bridle,
    and turned her inside.

Went to the house,
Mom said,
    "Hello."

I said,
"If anybody milks those cows tonight,
it's sure not going to be me."

*"There's a cougar in the pasture over there,
that cockeyed cougar's there!"*

I let the cows go that night.

There was some neighbors,
had a boy and a girl,
good big kids,
practically grown.

The girl went one night.
She was going a-milkin'.
There was a trail
went down from the house,
kind of zig zag like,
then the pasture was down there.

By gosh,
she started to get down
the cows one night.
She said
that darn cougar followed her
all the way back up the hill.
She'd look back
just about one turn
on this zig zig trail behind her.
He was following her.

By gosh,
somebody finally killed it,
but it had killed a bunch of stock.

Del also told some stories about wild animals that told of the
ranch hands being so adept at roping that they roped creatures such as
bears, deer, and coyotes. These stories indicated the high value that Del
and the other cowboys put on the skills of accurate roping aim, and

horsemanship. Del was very fond of the following brief description of some of the local boys roping a bear, and must have felt it would impress me, for he repeated it to me on all of my five recording sessions.

"Hanging the Bear"
Del Ringer, 1979

There was a bunch of boys.
They was wild devils.
        Come into the head of Wolf Creek one day
                and run on a bear.
He was in the spring.

Joe said to Al,
        "Let's rope him."

Al said,
        "Ok."
Joe caught him around the neck,
said,
        "Well, now we'll hang him."
He run a big limb that stuck out
        on the old tree,
        and Al grabbed it.
Took his dolly and
        took off and
by gosh,
        they hung the bear alright.
That tree,
        everybody in the country would laugh
        about that tree
        Al and Joe hung a bear to.
Called it, "The Hanging Tree."

It would appear that this incident became the basis for a commonly repeated story since the tree was named because of it. The boys must have gained local approval for their stunt and Del obviously must have admired their feat since he felt it bore repeated telling. Del, himself, was no slouch of a roper for he told me of his roping a coyote and a deer. Since the deer got the best of him, I guess he wasn't as proud of these encounters. He told me this story about roping the coyote and deer only once as a tag-on to the "Hanging the Bear" story.

"Del Ropes a Coyote and a Deer"[1]
Del Ringer, 1979

I never roped a bear, but
   I roped a coyote one time in the winter.

My gosh,
the snow was pretty deep.
He couldn't turn very fast
   and I run up to him on my horse
   and roped him.

He had the horse pretty much
   all tangled up,
   and finally when he come under my horse
so I could get the rope straightened out.
I took off
and drugged him to death.

Another time I roped me a buck deer.
I'll tell you
   that thing nearly whipped me to death!

It was about a four point buck, and
I was on a good horse,
   so I thought I'd rope him.

He was running down the ridge.
He come out on the range, and
   was going out on the range.

My cousin and I
   was ahead of him,
   was going to turn on the range,
 and my gosh,
   there was the buck.

I laughed
and said,
    "Watch me rope that deer."

He didn't think
    I could get that close to him.

But I run up on him
    and dropped that rope around his horns
and boy,
        when that rope tightened up the horn,
        he was first one way,
and then another,
and that horse couldn't turn fast enough.

I had welts all over my legs.

He's come to the end of the rope,
and it was snapped down on my leg.

And that horse had
all over his rump,
        welts as big as my thumb.

Finally,
        he was making it so hot for me,
I decided
        the heck with him.

I throwed my saddle off
and let him go.

I never did find him.

The point of the story was that even though he lost the deer, he obviously felt this was a pretty adventurous thing to attempt. He noted his cousin didn't think he could do it, as might the listeners. I sensed what must have been community approval for folks like Del and the boys who attempted such bold things.

Chapter Six:
Indian Stories

Them Indians was all peaceful. Some of the best friends
I had in that country was Indians.

—Del Ringer, 1973

Chief Joseph was a genius. People around here are still
studying his war tactics. He was a genius. He give up
on war.

—Delbert Wicks, 1985

Del Ringer frequently discussed how his family and neighbors all grew
up side by side with the Nez Perce Indians. Del said that when the
Indians would come into their place at Slate Creek every fall to camp
and hunt, his dad would pasture their horses. The Indians would buy
a side of beef and the squaws would keep busy with it while the men
were hunting. Del related, "They would salt it, and smoke it up over a
fire in the wickiup. Then they take it out on a block and pound it flat
and take it with them for the winter."

Indian Camp at Slate Creek 1877
Photo Grangeville Bicentennial Museum

Del's dad sold the Nez Perce deer hides which they made into gloves, moccasins, and boots that Del liked to wear. Del said:

> Dad and I used to wear them Indian boots in the wintertime over a pair of light socks. We'd work feeding cattle, slopping around; your feet just sweat. And you take them gloves. As long as you wore a dry pair, just keep your hands as warm as can be. Get wet, just throw them under the stove and put on a dry pair.

Del also remarked about the beautiful beadwork on the items he'd get from the women. "Them moccasins was beaded on the toes—flowers or deer or some damn thing. I'd always get Mom and Martha a pretty pair of beaded moccasins, and beaded gloves."

Nez Perce women
Courtesy Idaho Historical Society

One story that Del told on four storytelling occasions was "Old Peter Mox Mox." A great horse-swapping story, it reminded me of the dog-swapping stories in Richard Bauman's "Any Man Who Keeps More'n One Hound'll Lie to You." Del's story about Peter Mox Mox certainly seemed representative of a long tradition in American humor, i.e., the predilection for expressive lying. Bauman says:

> These stories told by hunters and traders are part of a long tradition of tall tales and personal experience narratives that have given American Folklore some of its most distinctive flavor.[1]

"Old Peter Mox Mox" [2]
Del Ringer, 1973

There was a horse trader
    come down the Salmon one year.

I had a little bay mare.
He had one.
They were just dead mates for each other.

He had a black and white spotted horse.
Well,
I wanted that horse.

He stopped at our place.
Had his horses in our pasture
    for three or four days
    to rest up, you know
He wanted that little bay mare awful bad.

I said,
    "What do you want for that spotted gelding there?"
    (He wanted seventy-five dollars for him.)
I said,
    "I won't give your seventy five dollars for him."
I said,
    "I'll trade you that little bay mare."
He said,
    "I'll trade you for twenty dollars to boot."
I said,
    "Not with me."
Finally he said,
    "I'll trade you for ten dollar."

    "Nope," I said.
    "I'll just trade even with you."
He monkeyed around until the morning he left.

Said,
    "I'll trade with you."

I think he didn't want me to get hold of the old horse,
because he had been spoiled,
    and didn't want me to try him out
        while he was around there.

So he was all hitched up and ready to go.
He said,
    "I'll trade you the horse for the little bay mare.
    I'm taking a rookin' on it, but I want her."

    "Then everything is ok."
I said,
    "An even trade."

So he left the spotted horse,
    and took the little bay mare.

When he was gone, I saddled the horse up,
    (very gentle acting devil.)
I got him
and tried to ride him away from the barn there,
I couldn't get him
    away from the barn.

There was some wild horses
    in the barn he'd been running with.
He wouldn't leave.

I spurred him.
Tried to get him going,
    and he'd just rare up.
He'd prettinear go over backwards on me.

So I kept after him,
    and finally got him
    away from the barn.

But you just saddle him up with a horse
    he'd been used to running with,
    and somebody was on it with you,
why you couldn't find a nicer horse to ride.

So I decided
    I didn't want him bad as
    I thought I did.

Them Indians,
    any pretty pinto,
    or appaloosa,
    or sorrel,
    that they'd see,

and by gosh,
    they'd want that one.

Old Peter Mox Mox,
    come in one fall.
I showed him this horse.
Made it a point to be around
    with this horse.

Peter said,
    "I want this horse.
    How much?"

I said,
    "One hundren 'n twenty-five dollars."
(Gosh,
    at that time you could buy
    a damn good horse for fifty dollars.)

Peter said,
    "I haven't got
    one hundred 'n twenty five dollars with me.
    All I have is seventy five dollars.
    I'll buy the horse if you'll trust me
        until I get down to Lap Wai to the Agency,
        so I can get the money."
I said,
    "Sure,
    you're good for it, Peter."

So he took it.
    I let him have it for seventy-five dollars.

He had two or three girls.
So he wanted him for his daughters.

He saddled the horse up,
    and tried to get him out.
He prettinear fell over backwards,
    two or three times on Peter.

He said,
    "I guess he don't want to leave home.
    I'll lead him."
He took the saddle off, and
    put it on another horse.
He went off leading him.
So next fall
    when he come back,
he didn't have the spotted horse,
    and I asked him,
"Where's the spotted horse, Peter?"
"Oh," he said,
    "I think maybe he die."
(I think he killed the spotted horse.)

Spotted pony along the Salmon River
MHB 1994

I had witnessed so far in Del's stories, a wealth of ironic humor and marvelous characters. While I never learned much about their appearance or their backgrounds, I gained a good sense of their personalities through his use of dialogue. Del, the trader, and Peter Mox Mox were sketched as the main characters in the two horse-trading conversations. Both conversations seemed ironic because in each case, one of the parties knew that this was a bad horse, and pretended not to want to sell it. In the second conversation the listener had become aware as well, and this made for humor. Del portrayed himself as a skillful horse trader, but not an infallible one, which we learned as he, too, got taken once in a while. The detail continued to be minimal in that there was just enough told about the trader and Peter's situation for the story to make sense. Thus, the story partook of Del's sparse telling style with dialogue highlights, and of course, his simple vocabulary and regional speech choices like "prettinear" and "gosh."

The attitude that was conveyed in the Peter Mox Mox episode was that if you made a bad horse swap, the best thing to do was to pass it on to someone else like an unsuspecting Indian. The moral was that one should be on one's guard when horse-trading as it is a fine art even for an expert like Del.[3]

Del told me the "Mox Mox" story on all five occasions that I recorded him. It remained quite stable in all its versions, and always included the two trading situations and the "maybe he die" ending. On three occasions, Del included a priceless description of Peter's preaching. This preaching episode was one that Del rendered convincingly with an imitation of Peter's preaching voice.

"Peter Mox Mox Preaches"
Del Ringer, 1982

He was religious,
    Peter Mox Mox.
Them Indians was all religious.
They wouldn't hunt on a Sunday.
One Sunday he wanted to know
    if I wouldn't come to church.

    "Sure, I'll come."

    "Young man,
            young woman,
    when you get up to heaven,
    everything good up there.

    Good shirt,
    Good pants.
    Good coffee!"

(By gosh,
I just about burst out laughing,
but he was just as serious as he could be.)

    "Good shirt.
    Good pants.
    Good coffee."

He was saying,
    "Don't put your money in the bank.
            You don't know where it goes.
    Put it in your pants pocket.
            You know where it is."

Del and his family, while it might not appear so in "Old Peter Mox Mox," were actually quite sympathetic toward the Indians, as you will learn in the following story he related about the Nez Perce War of 1877.

"The Indian War"
Del Ringer, 1979

There is a story that I'd like you to hear.
    A story of the Indians.
We read articles about the Indian War,
    but it wasn't anything
    like the way grandmother told it.

Ruth's mother and I,
    we always favored the Indians.
    Took their part.

When they took Old Chief Joseph and his tribe,
they had about 1000 head of cattle,
        and 1500 head of horses.
White men wanted that country.
Never had anything to do with it,
    just the Indians.

They called Old Chief Joseph to come.
Took the Indians almost a week to make the trip.
Called 'em over there.
Said they'd give 'em two weeks to vacate,
and if they didn't,
    they were going to send troops in.
Had twenty-five thousand head of livestock.
They got what they could.

It was spring.
The Snake and the Salmon,
    both rivers was high
so they ferried across.
The men could swim across the river with horses,

but the women and kids,
they just put on old dry cowhides,
      and towed 'em behind the horses.

They gathered up part of the horses and cattle.
They took what they could,
      and the rest they just left behind
      and the white men took 'em over.

When they got to the other side,
      after they had crossed the Salmon,
they started down the river.

There was two men at Slate Creek.

They wanted them horses
      when they come to Slate Creek.
The old fellow,
      he'd always been friendly with the Indians,
said,
      "No, boys, we won't give 'em up."

It was a log cabin.
They only had one rifle
but said,
      "You boys start any trouble,
      we got lots of guns and ammo here,
            and a bunch of you boys be killed."
So they went on, and left them.

They went on up to the mouth at White Bird Creek.
There was a family called Benedict.

Some of the young bucks started
      whooping and hollering.

Benedict had two horses.
Mrs. Benedict got on one of 'em.
      She had the baby.

Then the little boy
  and the dad, Mr. Benedict,
  got on the other.

They started up White Bird Creek.
The young bucks shot him in the back
  and captured the boy.[4]

Mrs. Benedict got away.
  Got up by White Bird.

There was a big corn patch,
  and she hid out for two days
  in the corn patch with the baby.

It got to crying
  and finally they found her.
She said she could hear the Indians
  going back and forth in the corn patch,
  and see 'em every once in awhile.
She managed to keep out of sight,
  but the baby got to crying,
  and they captured her.

She was a Catholic.
The Indians had a lot of respect for the Catholics.
Took her and cut a cross on each of her knees.
Then took her prisoner near Grangeville,
    about a mile and half from
    where the white men was camped.

There was a fort.
  Had an old log fence.
  Didn't have no cover on it.
Was high enough
  this old Irishman
  could stand up, and look out the top.

The Indians never came within a half mile of
  this so called fort.

The Irishman said,
    "I'm going out to get Mrs. Benedict."

They tried to get him not to go.
    "Well," he said,
    "they won't bother me."

He walked out to where the Indians was camped,
    and when he got to within hollering distance,
he hollered,
    "Joseph, come out,
    I want to pow wow with you."

So Joseph came out,
    wondered what it was.
Irishman unbuttoned his shirt.
He had a chain, with a cross on it.
    Throwed it back.
    Showed the cross.
Joseph came out, and talked to him awhile.
The young bucks, they wanted to kill him.
Joseph said,
    "No, he is a brave man.
    You stand back."

"We want Mrs. Benedict,
    and we're going to take her."

Her legs were so sore
    from the crosses on her knees,
    she couldn't walk.
So he just picked her up,
    and carried her back to Mount Idaho
    right into the fort.

From there they went across that old pass.
The Indians outsmarted the white men all the way.
Got over into Montana,
    a place where they camped all night.

I don't remember what general came.
    He stayed a day behind them.
The white soldiers
    went into Joseph's camp one morning.
They wouldn't go anywhere in the evening.
They waited until the next morning.
    Laid in the bush.
Next morning when the squaws came out,
    they shot the squaws.
When the little papooses came out of their wickiups,
    they shot them too.

Joseph and some of 'em got away.
They were just about to get
    some of their wives and kids,
    and get 'em across to Canada
        where they couldn't do nothing about them.
But another bunch of white soldiers come.
    So Joseph had to give up.

I don't think the Indians were any more brutal,
    than the white men.

Chief Joseph
Courtesy Idaho State Historical Society photo by 1887-E

Isabella Benedict Robie
Photo Granville Bicentennial Museum

This second Indian story was one of the few serious stories Del told. It provided the clear indication to me that Del was capable of varying his personal style to fit the style of the story. "The Indian War" seemed a different story genre than the personal experience stories and local character anecdotes that comprised most of his repertoire. It was a family version of an oral history story. Del related the complete version in September of 1979. In November of 1973, he told me a condensed version which included only the story of Mrs. Benedict's rescue, without the story of Chief Joseph's attempt to escape from the pursuing soldiers.

This was the longest story I recorded from Del. Unlike most of the other stories, he attributed this one to someone else. He said he heard the story from his grandmother Hannah Rice, who was told these events by Mrs. Benedict. Del was anxious to correct "a mistaken account" of Mrs. Benedict's story that he had read in the newspaper. I later discovered that this mistaken account in the paper had been provided by Alice Robie Mahurin, Mrs. Benedict's granddaughter. I include Alice Mahurin's version in a later chapter.

Del's story seemed designed to enlist our sympathy for the Indians. The listener was given a description of how the Indians crossed the river with considerable difficulty and loss of stock. In the later version,

Del related, Mrs. Benedict said one of the Indian squaws saw her in the cornfield but pretended not to see her, and told the braves it was an Indian baby crying so that they would not find Mrs. Benedict. Del's description of the soldiers shooting the squaws and the papooses as they came out of their wickiup was heartrending.

There were no examples of the irony, humor, or exaggeration that were prevalent in his other stories. Del's telling of "The Indian War" partook of what John Ball calls "the style of the story."[5] Del must have realized that the ironic humorous cartoon style of most of his stories was not appropriate in this serious story about the war, and the reported "savage deeds" of the Indians. Del's story showed that the white settlers were not without blame.

In 1995, I visited Chief Joseph's grave on the Colville reservation at Nespelem, Washington. When Joseph surrendered he believed that he and his people would be allowed to return to the reservation at Lap Wai.[6] Instead, they were interned in a number of places. Joseph unsuccessfully pleaded their case in Washington, DC. He died on the Colville reservation in Washington and never saw his beloved Idaho homeland again after the war of 1877. I was moved by the many offerings and tributes on his grave including one placed there by Nez Perce high school students, which said, "Class of '95 will never forget you."

Chief Joseph's grave
Photo MHB 1995

Chapter Six Notes

[1] See Richard Bauman, "Any Man who Keeps More'n One Hound'll Lie to You," in *And Other Neighborly Names,* eds. Richard Bauman and Roger D. Abrahams (Austin and London: University of Texas Press, 1981), pp. 79–103.

[2] Ibid. p. 101.

[3] "Old Peter Mox Mox" could be indexed under K 134.6, "Selling a balky horse."

[4] For similar stories see Brunhile Biebuyck-Goetz, "This is the Dyin' Truth: Mechanic of Lying," *Journal of the Folklore Institute,* 14, pp.73–95, and Bill Ferris, *Ray Lum, Muletrader: An Essay,* (Memphis, Tenn: Memphis Center for Southern Folklore, 1977).

[5] A possible motive for the Indians' killing of Mr. Benedict is related by his son Grant Benedict in Robert G. Bailey, *The River of No Return,* (Idaho: The R. G. Bailey Printing Company, 1947), pp. 274–5. It appears that Benedict Sr. had killed some Indians the year before the Joseph outbreak during an attempted robbery of the Benedict store.

[6] See Ball, "Style in the Folktale," 72.

[7] See Bailey, *River of No Return,* 242.

Chapter Seven:
Conclusions on Del Ringer's
Storytelling Style

"Walnuts and Peppers"
Everybody said what a damn fool Old Henry Ricke
was. He had to use a crowbar to dig them holes to plant
them damned trees.
—Del Ringer, 1975

There are just two more Del Ringer stories I would like to share with
you before drawing a few conclusions about his storytelling techniques.
I chose them because they happen to be two of my favorite stories, and
his, too. Both are about agricultural products, walnuts and peppers. He
told "The Walnuts" at five of the recording sessions. In several versions
he called the hero Old Joe Bosley, but in the others he called him
Henry Ricke, which appears to be the correct name for his hero.[1]

"The Walnuts"
Del Ringer, 1973

Old Henry Ricke,
he was up between Riggins and Lucile
    on the Salmon.
He took a little homestead there,
    and there were rocks.

Gosh almighty,
That little old bar where he took homestead
   was rocky.

There was a little old creek come down,
well, during the night
   it'd dry up.

Old Henry set out a bunch of walnuts there.
God,
everybody in the county laughed at him
   setting out a bunch of walnut trees.

The first year they bore $1200 worth.

He laughed and said,
   "Henry Ricke ain't such a damn fool
      even if his clothes don't fit!"

He planted them damn trees,
A lot of 'em he had to use a crowbar
   to get down between the rocks.
Planted 'em in there.
I know.
We was up there.
   It's been six, seven years ago.
Went over to Martha's brother's,
   and up to the Salmon,
      and stopped there at Riggins.

But when we went by Old Henry's place
I told Roper,
   "I see where Old Henry lived."

The walnut trees was still there.
   I don't know who had the place.
Got to be pretty good sized trees.

He had a little old one room cabin.
Wasn't big enough to
   cuss a cat in!

Old walnut tree at Slate Creek
Photo MHB 1995

Little old cabin along Route 95
Photo MHB 1995

Most likely this story was not really a personal experience narrative. It probably was a widely circulated local character anecdote with the added personal reminiscence of Del's later visit to the orchard site. In any case, I noted it was insignificant in his telling style whether he witnessed an event first hand, or simply relayed it. His niece, Mary Auvil, also noted this tendency as she remarked in our interview in her home in Soquel, California, on January 2, 1986:

> I recall some stories that he wasn't in, rather just sort of an observer. I remember one about him being in a movie house and eels being caught in the flume. I'm not sure whether he was in the theatre or not. He might have been in the theater when it happened, but if so, he didn't play a part as a character in his story. It didn't matter much to the story.

Del's attitude about Henry Ritchie's planting the walnuts came through loud and clear. This was one of the few local character stories Del told where he expressed approval for a character. "The Walnuts" to me resembled the admiring reminiscence-type portraits of Maine down-easter characters included in Richard Dorson's *Buying the Wind.*[2] Del aligned himself with "Old Henry" rather than the foolish folk who ridiculed him. In the 1965 version, Del included this colorful quote from one of the foolish hecklers:

> That damn old fool!
> Why don't he take his money
> that he spent for those trees
> *and throw it in the river.*
> That's all it will ever amount to!

Del also included in the 1965 version some detail that really emphasized the difficulty of trying to grow anything on those steep hills around the Salmon. He quoted Henry as saying:

> I've heard of hill
> that were straight up and down
> but it's the first time,
> I've seen them
> that *you can't see to the top*!

Steep hills above the Salmon
Photo MHB 1995

Like in a classic fairy tale, Del showed that those who are simple and good at heart, who persist despite scorn and work hard to follow their dreams, will be rewarded. As Mary Auvil said, "In a way, I think they [his stories] are almost like parables." Personally, I must say, it gave me a thrill when I visited the Salmon River country in 1994 and 1999, and saw an old walnut tree that I imagined Henry Ricke must have planted. I visualized Henry strutting around heaven saying he's no damn fool even if his clothes don't fit.

Del told this last story, "The Pickled Peppers," on all six recording occasions, and it was one which his family reports he loved telling. All Del needed to get going on this one was a word from Martha like, "you know, tell her about the pickled peppers." I wanted to include it because, although most of his stories take place along the Salmon, a few are set in Buena, Washington, where the extended family moved in 1928 and lived for a few years after their attempts to make it homesteading along the Salmon failed. This seems to be the last locale that he used in storytelling. In 1936 Del moved to North Bend, Washington, where he spent the rest of his life, but for some reason North Bend never became a setting for his stories. I guess for him youth was the golden time he wished to relive in his stories.

"The Pickled Peppers"
Del Ringer, 1965

You know, Mary,
  there used to be when we over there in the valley,
they had dances at the Women's Club in Parker.

We used to,
  a bunch of us from Buena,
we used to go up to the dances,
  and they had a little movie Frenchman there.
He was the floor manager.

And by God,
they'd dance 'til midnight,
  and at midnight they'd quit dancing.

They'd bring in a table.
You'd stand up and take whatever you wanted.
Well,
and they'd make a big wash boiler full of coffee,
and they'd take about an hour out then, after midnight.

If you wanted to dance longer,
  the little Frenchman would jump up
        on the music stand on the stage
        and hold out his hat
and everything after midnight
        went to the orchestra, see.
God,
they'd dance around
  and throw in four bits, you know.
I knew a fellow played in that orchestra,
and he said,
  "Hell, we always get more after midnight."
God,
they'd play until four o'clock in the morning,
  if you wanted to, see.

Well,
the little Frenchman
    he never brought a lunch course
        'cause he was a bachelor.
He'd go around with that keg of peppers
    under his arm to everybody,
and say,
    "Here, have a pepper."
And he'd see a sandwich that took his eye
Old Joe would reach out and get the sandwich.
God,
in that keg they was mostly those big old,
        (not too big)
    but those green old bull nose,
        green sweet peppers,
        and red ones.
Every once in awhile somebody would get one,
Jesus,
how they would holler for the fire department!

Joe, would slip in a hot pepper, you know,
    and laugh then.
That darn little whelp
    would just laugh his head off
        when somebody got one of them.

They looked just like the others, you know,
but, *God almighty,*
    was them things hot!

You'd bite into one of them,
    and you'd jump up to

See if the bottom was still in your chair
    or if it had burnt it out!

They didn't have any law up there.
Two or three of the women had big husky husbands
    and they'd represent the law up there.

One time,
these Davis boys come up there,
    and was going to break up the dance.

Oh,
they'd got pretty well loaded themselves
    drinking on the floor in the hall.

By gosh,
    Joe was on them two guys right now.
They was both pretty good sized,
    and was bucking Joe trying to get away from him.
He took 'em outside
    clear out the hall.

Mike Blaedeau and I went outside after a bit.
Joe didn't come in
    and we thought maybe they had teamed up on Joe,
but we went out.

There was two cars.
Between the second and the third car
    I heard a ruckus.
We looked that way.
It was Joe.
He smacked one of those guys,
    knocked him down,
    and he was trying' to get up.
He hit the other one.
He was draped over the fender.
He said,
    "Don't hit me again."
He was just a-beggin'.
He was a good fellow.
Mike said to Joe,
    "You need any help?"

"No," he said.
"You guys could have probably
give me some help with them ."
But,
he just banged them guys right and left.
He told 'em when he'd give 'em a good trimmin'.
He said,
"You guys want to go back in the hall.
Ok, you can go in,
if you can behave yourself.
If you can't,
stop there at the ticket window,
and they'll refund your dollar."
They said didn't want the dollar refunded.
They wanted to go back in.
They come back in.

They was *perfect gentlemen*
from then on until the dance broke up.

Once Del added to the story this amusing episode about getting his gum tangled up in a blonde's hair:

There was a tall willowy dame.
She was a blonde.
I got a hold of her in the dance.
Her hair was right fine.
The door was open.
It was along in early spring.
There was a draft here in the hall.

We was a-dancin'.
She was one of those cuddly kind of gals,
laid her face right up to yours.

Had a chew of gum in my mouth.
The wind blew some of that hair in my mouth.
I got it chewed up with that wad of gum.

Just like that,
    that wad of gum slid out of my mouth.

She was around all evening with
    that wad of gum in her hair.

I bet she would have cussed me
    black and blue
when she finally discovered it!

What became clear was Del's attitude about these events. One sensed an attitude of acceptance toward pranks played on strangers, but not friends. Thus, in the 1975 version, Del was warned before he mistakenly took a hot pepper:

One night,
    I got a pickled pepper out of his barrel,

He said,
    "No, you don't want that one."

He whispers to me,
    "That's a hot one."

Another attitude expressed here was that rowdies who do not know how to behave properly at a dance should be taught a lesson. Good manners with ladies were important to Del.

I have more Ringer stories, some forty in all, but I believe I have shared a sufficient number of his stories to make these general observations about his stylistic preferences in storytelling. Let me summarize them briefly.

At the surface level of vocabulary and speech patterns, I consistently found that Del used a small number of concrete words to tell his stories. The most prevalent nouns were the names of the characters and the basic items necessary for the story. There was nothing distinguishable about these common words. The charm lay in what he did with them to create his country style humor, as in the statement, "the cabin wasn't big enough to cuss a cat in," or his unusual use of traditional expressions like, "cuss him black and blue." Even people used to cussing, find cussing black and blue a surprising twist. He had many favorite words that marked his style, such as "old" before names, "pretty," "prettinear," "by gosh," and "boy," as well as regional forms such as "a –bellerin." When the occasion allowed, he used some profanity such as "goddamn" or "damn crazy bitches," or the slightly off-color, "ass over teakettle."

At the second level of his literary framing, Del varied his style as appropriate to the story. The actual percentage of dialogue varied from story to story, but in all stories, dialogue was a strong feature because these lines served as highlights of the stories and were also used to help delineate characters. Another distinctive feature of his literary styling was the cartoon-like style; that is, his description was sparse but compelling, leading to the creation of scenes and characters in broad strokes rather than with precise detail. Also, he used repetition, which gave a poetic quality and rhythm to the stories. Occasionally he used a simile or metaphor, but the use of these did not mark his style. The use of exaggeration was prevalent. Irony used as humor seemed a critical marker of his style. Most stories involved the idea that someone knew something that someone else didn't.

In actual performance, Del's stories showed variation in length on different occasions, particularly when a second episode was added. There was no evidence to show that he embellished his stories with time. Del was definitely aware that he was performing and he enjoyed his reputation as a storyteller, and happily responded to any occasion allowing an opportunity to tell his stories. He always presented his stories dramatically, with full vocal and facial characterization. He did not use many gestures or larger movements. In his youth he may have had a more physically vigorous manner of presentation, but by the time I recorded him, Del had already suffered a stroke and was chair-bound. He used a slow, deliberate speaking rate, with significant pauses.

Finally, the stories were complete with his evaluative comments that served as vehicles for Del's attitudes and views on life. The themes and attitudes he presented I suspect were representative of those prevalent along the Salmon River in the northwest at the turn of the century. They undoubtedly have even wider distribution in worldviews expressed in other areas of the United States since I could index many of the stories with widespread folkloric motifs. Del's stories were full of scorn for bunglers, rowdies, and city-bred dudes. There was admiration for those who are brave in the face of danger, and for those who succeed through perseverance and hard work. We learned the marks of gentlemen who knew how to dance, behave, and talk with the ladies, and of the foolishness of those who lacked these abilities. We learned of appreciation for those who were skilled at common tasks, and who turned their professional skills into a bit of fun. We learned that practical jokes and trickery in swapping are ok with strangers, but not with the local folks. Above all, we learned that the adventures of life in those days were always good grist for story making.

Next, I would like to share stories from other tellers from this area. I sought them out because I wanted to learn if he was just a maverick North Bend logger who liked to reminisce about his youth, or was Del a storyteller whose techniques had been shaped by the Salmon River storytelling traditions he experienced in his youth.

Chapter Seven Notes

[1] See Carrey and Conley, *River of No Return,* 263. They indicate that apparently Henry Ricke lived at Crawford Bar for three decades, and that the famous walnut trees evidently survived until the new highway was built. When the water table was lowered it caused the trees to die.

[2] See Richard Dorson, *Buying the Wind* (Chicago: University to Chicago Press, 1964), pp. 65–77.

Part Two
The Salmon River Narrators

Chapter Eight:
Delbert Wicks

Too bad Old Loy Hollenbeak isn't still alive. He'd tell
you stories about the pranks they played on the green
horns come to work for the forest service.

—Delbert Wicks, 1985

The first interview I had when I got to the Salmon River country was
with Delbert Wicks. At the Stinker Store in Riggins, I caught the
attention of his son and daughter-in-law who volunteered to call him
and arrange for me to meet him after I told them of my quest for
storytellers. They described Delbert as a "great talker." I found this to
be true. The following morning, the last day of August 1985, I drove
to his place across the bridge that has made him famous in the region.
He called it "the Little Golden Gate." Just after he bought his place in
1948, the river took out the existing bridge, so he built this one which
has been widely copied. It is a suspension bridge across the Salmon. He
built it himself, using steel headers. The locals consider it an engineering
marvel. He says that before then most folks just threw down three or
four logs across a narrow point in the river.

The Little Golden Gate
Photo MHB 1986

Delbert's family settled in Midvale. His mother's folks came by covered wagon, while his father's came by train, renting a boxcar for the journey. Delbert was born in 1915. "I was born in one of them four-room antique frame houses my uncle built," he said. His great Uncle Sherman, a trader of wild horses, had a homestead on Crane Creek for them where he grew up

> When I was a kid back in the Depression, that was a rough one all right. I tell you one thing you really had to stretch out the dollar or you didn't make it. You could get a job for a dollar a day. A dollar went a ways but only so far. The women did a lot of sewing and canning. You didn't just run to town for this and that. And you really worked with your neighbors in them days. All the neighbors helped neighbors but then when they come out with machinery, got rid of that

Delbert left the Salmon for a stint in the army. Then after five years in the heavy construction business, Delbert married Lola Price and went into the sheep business near Riggins, leasing land for about two thousand ewes until his retirement. He said:

> I really enjoyed running sheep here. I was up there in the mountains all summer. We'd camp and fish. We used pack mules to run sheep. If you were working with them wild or ran-a-tan mules it could be a little dangerous. I wasn't much of a mule man. Mules are good travelers. They got a different gait than a horse. I never could get used to them after riding horses so much. I had dogs that would just herd them sheep themselves. In fact we used Australian shepherd and border collies. I like them crossed the best.

Delbert Wicks and his dog
Photo MHB 1985

Delbert's place near Riggins was rather tumbledown with old equipment lying around outside. He told me of the life of a sheepherder, the daily routine, and of the ways to preserve meat in an old wool blanket out on the drive. Into all this information he would weave an occasional personal experience story about various local characters, or his own adventures. Delbert knew the Jewetts and said of them, "Yeah, I knew old Bill Jewett and he had a daughter. They were old-time people. They never went no place. They was homebodies."

He had what I would call an understated style. For example, he related, "I come face to face with a cougar one time. That really excited me a bit. I was in shock and so was the cougar." Here is a sample story:

"Old Hollenbeak"[1]
Delbert Wicks, 1985

Old Hollenbeak
was quite a character.
He got burnt
and only lived a few days afterwards.
I was with Charlie Hall
(the guy I bought this place from).

Anyhow we went into town, and here's this guy.
He was getting old,
and he was tall,
and he was straight as a string,
and he had a beard.
And I said—
"Charlie," I said,
"who is that guy?"

Well, he told me his name,
and he lived out in the hills
all his life,
and moved into town
as he'd gotten older.
In fact, he had a dog,
and he'd buy that dog steak,
and he'd eat hamburger!

So Old Hollenbeak was out on the trail
going up to his cabin
and he had a fifty pound sack of flour
on his shoulder.

He said to him,
"Why don't you carry that flour
in front of you on the saddle?"

"Well," he said,
"I'm saving my horse."

View of Riggins in 1912 with Hollenbeak barn in foreground[2]
Photo Courtesy Grangeville Centennial Museum

With this first story I heard in the Salmon County I was immediately
reminded of Del Ringer's story about Jewett's saddle. The setting, i.e.,
meeting a fellow on the trail with his mule, the dialogue punch line,
and the ironic humorous attitude seemed very similar. Like the stories
of Del Ringer, the vocabulary was of ordinary, short simple words in
this story; Delbert used dialogue in the form of direct and indirect
discourse through the filter of his friend, Charlie Hall's mind. Delbert
related what Charlie told him as part of the background (Hollenbeak's
living in the hills and moving into town, and the part about the dog).
He used a little description as well, even a simile, as we learned he was

"straight as a string." There was irony, as everyone except Hollenbeak seemed to know that the mule was already bearing the weight of the flour. The line, "Old Hollenbeak was quite a character," told the listener Delbert's attitude toward the story.

Delbert used much vocal emphasis in telling the story, particularly changes in volume, emphasis, and rate. He laughed a lot, considering it very funny. It flowed with no interruptions and came in response to my question, "Who were some of the local characters?" Here already I found the same cultural attitude that was evidenced in Del Ringer's stories: these local characters made good subjects for entertaining stories.[3]

When Delbert began the next story, I knew I was on the right track. Here was another roping story. Who knows, maybe Del Ringer might have been the guy who roped the bear of whom Delbert speaks.

"The Bear"
Delbert Wicks, 1985

I knows guys that had roped elk,
and I know a guy that roped a bear.

Old Stepson,
over on Broadway.
He roped a couple of bear.
So anyway,
    they put one in a little pen
    at the sawmill at Pine Creek,
and they came on to the cow camp
about three miles or so.

Anyway,
they came back to the sawmill
next morning,
    and, of course,
    this old man that run the sawmill,
    he stayed up with that bear all night.

Bear wasn't acting too good;
they had hurt him
    when they had roped him,
and so this old Shopshire,
he was kind of a long drawn-out talker.

"Well," he said—

"You know,
He passed away
about four o'clock
this morning."

Delbert certainly couldn't be described as telling long-winded detailed stories with elaborate vocabularies. Again in his brief story he used extremely common words. He used the double subjects as Del Ringer did sometimes. His literary framing was simple. There was only a single line of dialogue, but it served as the punch line and the highlight of the story, sort of a hallmark of Delbert Wicks's style. He used understatement when he said, "he wasn't too healthy," to explain that the bear was dead or dying. The detail was sparse for he only included what was needed to advance the story. One exception was that he did tell us in three different ways in three sentences that the bear wasn't well, an example of elaboration.

The presentation features are what helped this story. Delbert really drew out that last line at a snail's pace so he had us laughing. Delbert made an evaluative statement later, which was separate from the story. He told me, "Bear stories or rattlesnake stories are just a bunch of hot air." Here is one of his rattlesnake stories:

Here's this fellow riding around the hill
and here's this snake up on the hillside.
He struck this guy's boot,
and he died from the rattlesnake bite.

And anyhow, of course,
here come another guy
two or three years later,

and he decides to wear them boots,
and there is still enough venom in there
    that he had to go to the doctor.

(But heck,
why they can't even bite
through them boots.)

Delbert Wicks's and Del Ringer's telling styles, of course, showed their differences. The biggest difference was that when Del Ringer was telling a story in his showing mode or dramatized mode, he was much more adapt at dialogue and vocal characterization. However, the dialogue lines Delbert Wicks included were dramatized fully. Thus, they did share the common practice of dramatization of dialogue lines.

They also shared the traditions of having fun at the expense of simpler characters, or even animals, and seeing one's own experiences as humorous and story material. They certainly shared a tradition of common subject matter. Del's roping stories seemed cast in much the same mold as Delbert's. The common traditional attitude evidenced in both tellers' stories appeared to be that roping a wild creature was a pretty gutsy thing to do, and a topic for a good story.

Delbert got a big kick out of telling me a story about his own sense of humor. It was a first-person narrative with him as the main character.

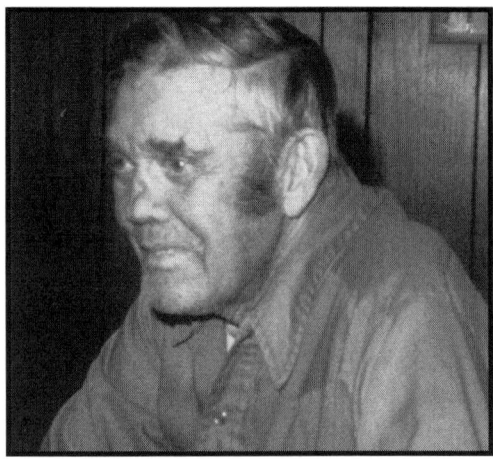

Delbert Wicks
Photo MHB 1985

"Muddy River"
Delbert Wicks, 1985

About thirty years ago, the ice blocked up the river,
and backed up water clear into town.

Why they didn't dynamite it
I'll never know,
the gol-dern-crazy knotheads!

Few people's houses and bridges washed out.
When that dern thing broke loose, did a lot of damage.
(This is kind of funny.)

The Circle C Ranch in New Meadows
had cattle all the way
from New Meadows to White Bird.
I had been feeding a few head
of sheep or cattle down here.
Me and this kid
crossed the bridge that morning,
and of course, the water had been way up.

(I'm always joking anyways.)

So here's the water all muddy.
So I says to that kid,

"They must have crossed cattle
up the river someplace."

Anyway,
before the day was over,
    he found out about the river!

There was only one line of dialogue in this simply told story, but,
as it was the clever punch line, it received much emphasis. There was
ironic humor, as Delbert and the readers or listeners knew full well that

the reason the water was muddy was because of the flood. Once again I found jokes and pranks played on the simpler as the source of humor. The detail in the story was brief, as in Del Ringer's style, and there was nothing that did not directly advance the story. There were no similes, metaphors, or other literary devices. One wonders, had he not been telling this in the presence of a lady, if the language might have been stronger than "gol-dern" and "dern."

This story was complete with evaluative statements like, "the gol-dern-crazy knotheads," "This is kind of funny," and "I'm always joking anyways." It flowed without interruptions. He used lively facial expression, lots of vocal variation, and plenty of his own chuckles. While Delbert was a vigorous storyteller, he was not as adept at dramatizing voices and creating a scene as Del Ringer.

He did resemble Del Ringer in his story patterns. The story about Old Hollenbeak on the trail was very similar to Del's story, "Jewett's Saddle." "Muddy River" was another joke on a greenhorn, like Del's "The Dude," and as we demonstrated, the "Roping a Bear" story appeared to be part of the roping wild animals tradition Del Ringer liked. Delbert Wicks's stories added support to my supposition that there were community storytelling traditions from this region, which influenced Del Ringer. I wondered if I would meet other tellers like Delbert Wicks. I didn't have to wait long to find an answer.[3]

Chapter Eight Notes

[1] "Old Hollenbeak" is related to J 1870, "Absurd sympathy for animals or objects" and J 1874, "Relieving the best of burden." It is also related to J 1041.2, "Miller, his son, and the ass." (In some variants, this tales ends with the miller carrying the donkey. The motive here is different though. He is doing this to try to please everyone.)

[2] There is a photo of Riggins in 1912 on page 135 of *Idaho County Voices,* which points out the Hollenbeak barn and also the old swinging bridge.

[3] A letter from Ron Mahurin in February of 1996 informed me that Delbert Wicks died January 10, 1988, and is buried in Midvale, Idaho.

Chapter Nine:
Gay Robie

I'm going to tell you about the guy on the
upper Salmon who roped the elk.
We know this guy so we know
this is true. This is true!

—Gay Robie, 1985

Delbert Wicks wanted me to meet Gay and Ralph Robie, and took me to their house later that day. Their home was as neat as a pin, and the grounds well kept. The interior was filled with many fine trophy antlers of deer and elk, as well as animal skins. Both Gay and Ralph wore western attire and were lean and youthful in appearance. They filled me in on their background.

Gay Robie, Ralph Robie, And Author
Photo MHB 1985

Ralph Robie and his sister, Alice Robie Mahurin, whom I met later, grew up and spent their lives along the Salmon. Ralph was born in 1920 and died in 1988. Ralph raised cattle on the South Fork and was a rodeo cowboy until his retirement in Riggins. At the time of my interview, Ralph and Gay had been married thirty-one years. They had no children. Gay appeared to be the storyteller of the family and Ralph deferred to her. I was delighted that I had found a woman storyteller.

Gay was born in 1915 and died in 1994. Her maiden name was Carrey. She came from a pioneer family who settled as sheep ranchers in a remote area on the South Fork near McCall. Cerreau, her grandfather on her father's side, came from Paris, France. He was, she said, "a sheep man who had nine children and died at an early age of pneumonia after a blizzard wiped out his five bands of sheep." Her mother came from Edinburgh, Scotland, as a young woman. She met her future husband and traveled from Oregon with him by horse and buggy. Gay managed to attend school as a child, along with her sister and brother, first by being boarded in town and later by riding a mule to school. When I asked what the family did for amusement when she was a child, Gay replied, "Well, in the evening when we was little we'd set around there and listen to the sheepherder, or whoever was there, tell cougar stories."[1]

Among her childhood memories was that of growing up with John Kimbrough, a bachelor whose thrifty ways enabled him to become a "walking bank." He was able therefore to save many a bankrupt rancher. John made his home with her family for twenty-five years. She said:

> What saved us during the depression was John Kimbrough. He herded sheep when he was a kid and saved every nickel. Then he got enough to buy a band of sheep. He didn't run sheep in our day, just backed people. He always carried a little briefcase. He in the Depression saved the ranchers that was saved here.

Delbert Wicks, who was present, added this example of John's thrift:

> He'd go around to these old sheep camps and find the dirty clothes that people would throw away when the camp tender would bring them new ones. He'd wash up those clothes. So he didn't even have to buy any clothes.

John Kimbrough, the walking bank
Photo courtesy Ace Barton
Signal American Printers

Gay found John Kimbrough somewhat eccentric, but kind to her and the other children, bringing them shoes and little presents when he returned from being away. "He liked custard pie for breakfast," she said, "so Mom always made custard pie for breakfast." Here is the account Gay gave of John's death:

"John Kimbrough's Death"[2]
Gay Robie, 1985

We was broke on the South Fork the first time,
    and he brought a guy, Louie Kowsky.
John Kimbrough brought Louie Kowsky in there
    to take over our ranch.
He had bought it from the bank.
John got to talkin' to my dad.

In them days you didn't take bankruptcy.
In them days my dad worked in the mines
    to pay off his debts, and his grocery bills,
    and the bank took the rest.

John Kimbrough took us up to Short Forks
    in the spring and set us up.
He was the most noted man in the country
    in the early days.
He lived until about seventy.

John always had a good bottle of whiskey,
    but he didn't go around treatin'.
He kept that bottle in the kitchen under the sink,
    and every night before he went to bed,
he put so much of that good whiskey in a glass,
    and he'd drink it before he went to bed.

He slept out on the porch,
    because that's where he liked to sleep.
A thunderstorm came up.

So Dad and Mom slept just inside.
So Dad said,

"I better go cover up John.
That wind's a-blowin' awful hard out there."

He went out there,
   and he was dead.
   Leakage of the heart.

So anyhow,
   he was dead right there.
So that was all there was to that.

So his briefcase he always carried,
   I don't think any of us
   ever did see inside it.

Well right then and there,
Dad put tape on it
   and took it.

Took it right to the bank.

John Kimbrough, the subject of Gay's personal experience narrative, was mentioned by others whom I met. Later I had the opportunity to interview his nephew Gus Carlson. I suspect there might be many other stories and legends about John Kimbrough in the Salmon River country, and hope to return someday on this quest.

Gay made it a point to be sure that everything she was telling me was true, and not just rumor. At one point I asked her if she knew any Sasquatch stories, and she told me that she had been in the same area at the same time as a reported sighting, but that it was "just a wild story" and that, "there couldn't have been very much in there, or the animals would have been spooked or something." Unlike Del, or Delbert, Gay was more interested in accuracy than in forming a good story. Regardless of whether Gay's stories were true or not, she told them engagingly and enthusiastically.

Here is her bear story, which she told as a personal experience narrative from her childhood:

"The Bear"
Gay Robie, 1985

My brother and I once
    was over on Partridge Creek.
Johnny and I,
    we heard a deer.
I used to tend camp a lot then,
    and the sheepherder,
he had to go out.
Sheepherders,
    you know,
when they want to go out
    and get drunk or something,
they get a bad tooth.

Johnny said,
    "Now you stop
    and tell Dad on your way out."
He said, "Ok."
Well, he never stopped
    and told Dad,
    and he left us in there for two weeks,
    and we run out of groceries
    and prettinear everything.
    and we didn't have our whole pack string in there
    and all,
    and it was getting awful,
        bear everywhere.

We got up one morning,
    and went to look for another place
        to take the sheep.
We were going up a draw like this,
    and Johnny had a gun you put a shell in,
    and we had a sheep dog
        that would have these running fits.
We started to cross the canyon,
    and I said to Johnny,
    "There's a cow."

Johnny said,
   "That's a bear."
It was about the reddest bear
   I ever saw in my life,
but anyhow about that time the dogs seen the bear
    and the dogs took off after the bear,
    and the bear ran around the hill,
    and run the dogs back,
    and every time runs the dogs back
        gets closer to us!

Johnny shove a shell in there,
   and he shot,
   and could see the bloody foam
      in that bear's mouth,
   and he hit her in the ribs.

We didn't know it then,
   but afterwards we found out
she had a cub up a tree right there.

So finally,
Johnny shoved another bullet in the barrel,
   and the shell stuck!
He couldn't get the shell either way.

So he says,
   "Run, Gay, run!"
I stood there,
   and just wet my pants!
I stood there,
   but then,
I passed Johnny on the way to camp!

That's a true story.

Anyhow, we got down,
   and we went back there the next day,
   and gathered up the gun,
   and the pocket knife,

and, of course,
the bear was gone.

Finally, Johnny had to go out.
John Phelan never told Dad nothing.

Her brother, Johnny Carrey, shared this adventure with her. Johnny is the well-known author of two local histories, *River of No Return* and *The Snake River of Hell's Canyon*,[3] the former with Cort Conley and the latter with Cort Conley and Ace Barton.

Gay, Mary, and John Carrey on their way to school, 1927
Photo courtesy Cort Conley

Gay's rapid, breathless presentation was a real contrast to Del Ringer and Delbert Wicks's slow, measured, relaxed styles. She had a tendency to keep her pitch high at the end of a sentence. At her speed there was no chance, or need, for interruption from the audience. It was obvious that Gay had related this story before.

The next story certainly appears to belong to a Salmon River family of roping stories.

"The Guy Who Roped the Elk"[4]
Gay Robie, 1985

I'm goin' to tell you
    about the guy on the upper Salmon
    who roped the elk.

We know this guy,
so we know this is true.
This is true!

So he had an awful good cowboy
    over there workin' for the forest service,
    and we'd sit up half the night tellin' stories.

Anyhow,
him and his relatives lived up there
    and he decided he wanted to rope an elk.

He had a truck you could throw a horse in.
So he went out there,
    and saw an elk,
    and roped him,
    and he had an awful time
gettin' the elk in the truck.

He got about half way home
    with that elk in the truck,
    and the game warden passed him.

So he hurried,
    and wanted to get rid of that elk,
but, no way
    could he get that elk
    to come out of the truck.

He shrieks and he hollers.
He did everything,
    but the game warden caught him,
and it cost him three hundred dollars.
He didn't want to rope no more elk!

By the time we got to this "true" story, Gay was on a storytelling roll. She volunteered to tell it as soon as Delbert had completed his story of the bear who passed away. Like Del Ringer, she shared that folks there talk about local characters and their adventures for amusement. As Gay said, "We'd sit up half the night telling stories." I imagine this story came out of such sessions; it seems so well-honed. Gay proceeded without pauses or interruptions except for our laughter and hers. She obviously viewed it as a story, a true story. She was careful to justify the source to whom she attributed the story; "We know this guy, so this is true." Her story was clean, devoid of profanity, and totally ladylike in her telling.

Here is one of Gay's "Cougar Stories" that might have been told at their storytelling sessions, "in the evening when they'd sit around tellin' cougar stories."

"The Deef Boy"
Gay Robie, 1985

There was a family used to come down
    that had a whole bunch of kids,
when we lived at the Frank Smith place.
Come to pick cherries.

We had cherries, and they didn't
    and I remember them a-comin',
    and I can remember one incident.
(I can barely remember this,)
But anyhow,
Mom had got dinner,
    and they come on the horses,
    and they had one boy
    that was deef and dumb.
He was a mute.

Anyhow,
I'm not sure whether he was deef or not,
but anyhow,
they was picking cherries,
    and Mom got dinner,
    and had 'em all come in for lunch.

Whatever this boy's name was,
they went out and hollered for him,
    and he didn't come,
    and the mother said,
    "Well, he's over at the bank
    going to the bathroom probably."
So they didn't pay too much attention to him like that.

They went looking again,
    and they never did find that boy,
    and the men,
    a posse come down and hunted,
    and my dad
    was in that, of course.
They tracked him across the Smith Creek,
    and up on that bare hillside back of the place,
    and went around in circles,
    and there was cougar tracks
    went around in circles.

The cougar must have carried him off.
They never found that boy.
My dad ran sheep in there two or three years later,
    and found a shoe.
Anyhow,
    that's a true story.

This story was another of Gay's childhood memory stories. She saw so few other children socially that when any visited she remembered the occasion well, as in this story. She did not reveal her feelings about the loss of the boy. Once again I heard the statement, "that's a true story," which indicated the importance to Gay that her stories were true, and also that she recognized this experience as story material. The attitude that life on the frontier could be a frightening and dangerous experience for children was only implied.

Gay, while sharing common traditions of story subjects, regional vocabulary, and attitudes with Del Ringer and Delbert Wicks, definitely had her own style of telling a flowing, melodious narrative, as she intoned the story with a steady beat and rhythm. There was never any question that Gay was a performer of these stories. She was very enthusiastic in telling the stories at a rapid pace while putting her whole body into the telling. Her presentation encouraged me to believe that storytelling has always been a favorite pastime in the valley, as she made numerous references to past storytelling occasions. Gay's subject matter was very much in line with the two men's stories as she told of encounters with wild animals, a roping story, and stories of local characters. Both Gay and Ralph have now passed on. When I visited White Bird in 1999, local folks spoke admiringly of them both and their legacy to the Salmon River stories.

Chapter Nine Notes

[1] These activities resemble those discussed in "The Family Saga as a Form of Folklore," in *The Family Saga and Other Phases of American Folklore*, by Moody C. Boatright, R. B. Downs, and J. T. Flanagan, (Urbana: University of Illinois Press, 1958), pp. 1–19.

[2] These Gay Robie stories appeared in M. Bennett, "Windy Stories from the Salmon River," *Northwest Folklore*, Vol. 7, Number 1 Fall 1988, pp.14–21.

[3] See Carrey and Conley, *River of No Return,* and Carrey, Conley, and Barton, *The Snake River of Hell's Canyon.*

[4] "The Guy Who Roped the Elk" is related to X1003, "Lie: remarkable roper."

Chapter Ten:
Alice Mahurin

Grandma Large said if you sew on a Sunday, you would
rip out every stitch in the other world with your nose.

—Alice Mahurin, 1985

Ralph Robie suggested that I talk to his sister, Alice Robie Mahurin,
who lived with her son, Ron Mahurin, a road construction worker,
near Slate Creek. I was excited about meeting them since I had learned
that the Mahurins lived near the Ringers' old place in Slate Creek, and
that Alice Mahurin had gone to school with Del Ringer. Happily, Alice
and Ron were at home and were very hospitable. At the time of my visit
in September of 1985, they were living in their old home, supposedly
the oldest house in the county.[1]

Ron and Alice Mahurin
Photo MHB 1985

Alice Mahurin was born in 1913. At the age of six months, Alice said she fell out of a buggy with a runaway horse while her mother was driving. She related to me the family story of how Old Doc Foskett, and a doctor from Walla Walla, performed an operation on her forehead on the kitchen table. She pointed out to me her flattened forehead as evidence for this story as she related:

> I was in a buggy accident once. The horses ran away. I fell out. I have a forehead that shows the scar. Old Doc Foskett operated on the kitchen table. They told my mother not to let me sleep on my back, but they couldn't keep me off, so my forehead kind of sunk in a little.

She said her father, Edward Robie, rode back so furiously to be there that his horse died upon arrival. Her son Ron had obviously heard the story before. He added to his mother's story, the remark that the Walla Walla doctor was a little high when he arrived, and that Old Doc Foskett made him go out to the barn and sleep it off before they did the operation.

Alice Robie Russell, Edward Victor Robie, and Emily Robie Chamberlain
Photo Grangeville Bicentennial Museum

Alice's paternal grandmother was the Mrs. Benedict who appeared as the heroine of Del Ringer's story, "The Indian War." Mr. Robie, Mrs. Benedict's second husband, was Alice's grandfather, the "Irishman" Edward Robie, who rescued the Widow Benedict from the Indians according to Del Ringer.[2] Her Grandfather Robie came to Idaho from Missouri after serving in the Union Army. He was a successful gold miner and as a bachelor had also worked on the Nez Perce Reserve at Lap Wai. Some years later, Grandfather Robie died on the trail of a heart attack while en route to Mount Idaho to fulfill his duties as county commissioner. He is buried on the Russell place, named after the son-in-law who later took over Robie's property.

Alice's other grandparents were Samuel Large (who Alice said was a small man) and Mary Purcell Large.[3] Alice related that Irish-born Mary came from Boston to join her husband. Finding no room on the stage from Grangeville, the newlyweds walked to White Bird to his bachelor one-room log cabin. Sam Large operated a mine at Large Bar on the Salmon about one and a half miles from Slate Creek. Their children later bought up the Harrah and Jewett homesteads. Alice recalled the holidays at her Grandmother Large:

> At the holidays we had a huge dinner with the neighbors at Grandmother Large's house. She'd order the stuff from E. S. Bergen Company in Spokane. It would come on the stage. You wouldn't believe the groceries that came with their special things for the holidays. You know sweet potatoes and things like that. We only had little presents at Christmas, just had a big dinner. Grandmother Large was known to make the best apple pie around.

Alice also shared memories about her dad in the days when she was growing up on the ranch. She said:

> My dad was one of the best riders in the country. He used to ride for the government when they would come and buy horses. He would bet with them when he got on the horses. Put a half dollar under the stirrup, and bet them that it would be there when he got through riding. He was never bucked off or lost a bet.

At an early age, Alice lost her father when he was dragged to death after catching his foot in the stirrup while mounting a horse. She described his death simply:

> My dad was killed by a horse. He was bucked, down by the thorn bush. He hadn't completely got on, got his foot caught in the stirrup, drugged him to death. I think I was only about six, seven.

This was one of the great sorrows of her youth, she said. After his death her mother kept up the ranch with her children. Her brother Ralph became a well-known rodeo performer. She said her brother Peck (Ben) got his name because, "when he was little, he was redheaded and just full of mischief, and my grandmother nicknamed him Peck's bad boy."

In 1937, Alice married Walter Mahurin and they lived for a few years in Spokane before returning to Slate Creek. Alice told me about her husband's stepmother, Katherine Boderick Mahurin, who taught in many of the local schools including Riggins, Slate Creek, and Banner Ridge near White Bird. Katherine lived to be one hundred and five. Katherine got lost coming home from school as a small child back in a South Dakota snowstorm. Alice said:

> She and a little boy were right within seeing distance of the house. She covered 'em up in a snow drift. Little boy froze to death. She froze her limbs, this finger off one hand, and one ear, but she wore her hair kind of in a pug behind and kept it covered. Teaching school she never had any discipline problems. She could keep up with any kid. Kick 'em in the butt with her artificial foot.

Katherine Mahurin, early teacher
Photo courtesy Granville Bicentennial Museum

Her husband died when Ron was sixteen, and Alice continued to live in the old house with her son. Both Alice and Ron turned out to be excellent storytellers who prided themselves on being experts on local history. Alice recalled well Clay Davis, the Berlinghoffs, the Jewetts, and other folks that Del Ringer had storied about. Ron is still consulted as a source for information about the area and its pioneers.[4]

Alice retrieved old albums of photos to show me. One, she pointed out, was a picture of Mrs. Benedict (later Robie) and her two sisters. Alice said:

> That's Grandma Robie on the left. She was quite plain. See here's a picture of her with her two sisters from New York. They had a saw mill back in New York, and then they came out here.

Mrs. Benedict and her two sisters
Photo courtesy Alice Mahurin

There was a picture of Edward Robie, her rescuer and second husband.

> This is a picture of my Grandfather Robie. He had a heart attack on the trail. He and a boy of his is buried

down on the Russell place. They was going to move'm to the cemetery but they were afraid 'cause the boy died of scarlet fever.

Edward Robie, rescuer of Mrs. Benedict
Photo courtesy Alice Mahurin

There was also a very interesting photo of a sketch that appeared in the local newspaper.[5] It was a picture of an Indian on a horse and a woman who Alice said was her grandmother, the very Mrs. Benedict that Del Ringer had told about in his story about the Nez Perce War. I was anxious to see how Alice's story about Mrs. Benedict's rescue by Grandpa Robie compared to Del Ringer's version.

"The Indian War"
Alice Mahurin, 1985

Mrs. Benedict.

The Indians came by.
Three chiefs, I think
    and they went in
    and talked to them.

My aunt told me she were eight years old,
   and the folks sent her in the bedroom
   and the Indians called her back out,
   and took off his belt which was all bloody,
   and made her wash the blood out of it.
It was hard to get off
   because it had dried on there,
   and she had quite a time trying to get it off.

They visited awhile,
   the Indians did,
   and then they left.
They later came back.

Benedict,
he went to the window
   to see what they wanted,
   and they shot him.
He told her before he died
   to take the kids
   which was Frankie and Cad.
(Catherine, I suppose her name was.
She was the baby. She had to pack her.)
He told her to stay in the brush.

She had to go out
   and overheard the Indians passing;
so she hid,
and this little girl,
she were afraid of the bear.
They were at the watering hole,
   the spring.
She told her to "shhhhhh."
   The bears wouldn't bother her.

Anyways, the soldiers came by then,
   and they had a battle at White Bird,
   and he were one of them.

They had to have a horse.
The rider had been killed on it.
It might have been gentle,
    but it was spooked.
They left her with this horse,
    but it bucked her off.
So she was left horseless,
    and she was a-makin' her way up river
    when this Indian came back by.

Grandma Robie had learnt his mother
    how to bake bread.

So he told her if she never told who he was
    he'd take her back by White Bird Creek
so she could hide in the brush,
so the Indians wouldn't know.
So she never did tell
who the Indian boy was.

She worked her way out,
    and went out
    and hid in an old barn by the prairie.

Robie, he came back and found her,
    and took her to Mount Idaho.

She was frightened,
    and was hiding in this barn
    and wouldn't come out
    for fear of the Indians.
            I have a picture that come out of the paper.[5]
It's just an imaginary one, of course.

My Aunt Alice Russell gave them the history.
She gave them this story,
    and it's correct,
    and I heard my Aunt Frankie tell it, too.

She married a fellow named Shissler.

Mrs. Benedict and a Nez Perce brave
Photo courtesy Alice Mahurin

I was stunned to hear in Alice's version of the story that Grandpa Robie only coaxed her grandmother out of a barn. Where was Del Ringer's episode of the daring rescue by the Irishman baring his cross and carrying her back across the lines? Both narrators claimed the story to be true and that they were told it by relatives who were in the position to know the truth. Alice Mahurin's Aunt Alice was Mrs. Benedict's daughter. Del's grandmother, Hannah Rice, was a good friend of Mrs. Benedict, and supposedly heard the story from her. Perhaps since Alice could claim the closer relationship, her story came closer to the truth.[5] When I told Alice about Del Ringer's version, Alice suggested Del might have gotten his story mixed up with one about a Mrs. Manuals, who supposedly got her tongue cut out by the Indians.[6] Said Alice, however, "I wouldn't want that put down as real history." Fortunately, the truth is not an issue here, only the comparison of storytelling styles.[7]

Besides the obvious content differences, one could spot some telling style similarities and differences between Alice and the other narrators immediately. Alice used the small vocabulary of ordinary words I had come to expect, with some colloquial forms such as "a-makin'" and "learnt." She consistently used "were" for "was," unlike Del or the others. Alice used more repetition than the others, particularly of the sentence patterns using the words "and" and "so." These repetitions added a distinctive personal rhythm to her story. Uniquely, she told the story totally in past tense. In its framing there was no dialogue, as in Del's version, in which to use present tense. There was only one direct quote, the sound "shhhh." There was a hint of indirect discourse in "the bears wouldn't bother her." Like Del, she chose significant details to highlight in description. There were no examples of irony.

Alice's story could be classified as a local history account. Her admiration for the courage of Mrs. Benedict and her rescuer was only implied. The listeners had to figure out the point of the story. Yet, as Sandra Stahl points out, a story can "function to teach the listener what the storyteller believes."[9] Like Gay Robie, Alice was very concerned that we realize this story as the truth, hence the attributions to both her Aunt Alice and Aunt Frankie.

Alice's oral presentation lacked sparkle. She had a soft, monotonous, and muffled voice, but she was very enthusiastic about telling this story and others to us. Alice did not require much urging to volunteer them. The stories were at her command so readily. I had the impression that she and her son often told stories of the old days.

Next, I asked Alice if she knew the Jewetts, and she replied with this story.

"The Jewetts"
Alice Mahurin, 1985

They were a different family.
They lived by the creek here.

I don't know—
the old man Jewett,
he was picking raspberries or something.
They always figured a snake bit him.
He died.
The family said a bee stung him.

The old lady and Bill lived there then.
In later years when Ronnie was little,
    they'd walk down.

They'd raised a little girl,
(that was Preston Jr.,)
and took her
and raised her when she was about a year.

They used to come over,
and instead of opening the gate,
they'd climb over!
The old lady was getting up there.
I guess it was just to show people she could.
When she got older,
    one of the daughters took her.
Well, they lived up there so long,
    I guess they got their own ideas.
They moved to Juliette then.
    I suppose she wasn't so well.

They went huckleberrying—
the daughter, the mother, and Old Bill.
The daughter's husband told her—
    he should stay at the pick-up with her.
But she told him,
No, to go on down there to the berry patch
to get his berries.
That's what they come for.
She'd be all right in the pick-up.
They had a bed or something fixed up in the back
    so if she wanted to lay down she could,
but she disappeared.
They never knew where she went.
They got the bloodhounds in.
The bloodhounds just went to the end of the road,
and never found her.

Old Bill came home.
He told me he often rode out there, thinking
        that the old lady would try to come home
but he never could find her,
    or know what became of her.

Just perished.
I imagine if the law knew what became of her
    they never told the public.

It was thrilling for me to find another Jewett story. Obviously Alice knew the same story I had heard from Del about the rattlesnake bite killing Old Jewett. She told a simpler version than Del did, and she preferred not to use dialogue. Her indirect discourse statements were filtered through several steps and minds. Del did not use techniques such as this. Alice's indirectly quoted scenes were the highlight of the action, however, and they carried the punch more than her descriptive lines. Though Alice related this story in her soft-spoken monotone pitch, it was not without feeling. Through volume and phrasing, she achieved some variation. A sense that she relished telling this story came through, and I realized that her monotone was just her characteristic speech pattern.

There were strong undertones of suggestions of foul play connected with this story. Later when the Jewett's gravestones were being discussed, Alice said, "They were out huckleberrying. When they came back to the pickup, somebody must have stolen her, 'cause the old lady were gone." Alice shared with me some suspicions about who might have "stolen her." She asked me not to record them, so I have respected her wishes. As Ron showed us the Jewett graves, he pointed out, "See Rose has got no date. She's the one that come up missing when they was out huckleberrying."

Alice's attitude about the Jewetts concurred with that of the various narrators I had met. That attitude appeared to be, that while all considered the Jewetts a source of entertaining stories, their pathetic deaths were tragic and unnecessary. Old Jewett died, we learned from Del Ringer, as the result of a rattlesnake bite because Jewett refused treatment, insisting it was only a bee sting. Ron Mahurin told me that Bill Jewett was said to have died when his horse fell down a canyon, but Ron indicated there was some suspicion locally that there might have been foul play involved here, too. We have seen that Alice suggested that Old Rose Jewett's death or disappearance was full of questions.

Old Man (Preston) Jewett and Rose Jewett's stones, White Bird
Photo MHB 1994

Alice's next story was about Johnny Nevins. I recognized his name as the fellow who had sold Old Jewett the roll of roofing paper in Del Ringer's "Jewett's Roof" story.

"Nevins's Death"
Alice Mahurin, 1985

Johnny Nevins,
he was up in front of the church.
They shot him.

Old Doc Foskett,
he was up at Skookumchuck,
    and his aunt had to go up
    and look for the doctor to come down.

They had a saddle mule,
    and it wouldn't go.
She had to drag him
    prettinear all the way down the hill,
    you know.

She got down there.
The doctor had already left
    to come to White Bird.
She went down over the hill,
    and he came down the road.

That was way back.

He's buried up there.
He's got a stone.

If this story, a little local history portrait, had dialogue in it, it could have been one of Del's, as the styles seemed close in many ways. In this short vignette the word choice and sentence structure were like Del's—short and simple. The use of "old" as a modifier is another usage they shared. Like Del, she used only sparse, well-selected detail, but one can visualize the dragging of the mule "prettinear all the way down the hill." There was repetition and rhythm in the sentence patterns that was reminiscent of Del's style. Unlike in Del's stories, however, it was more difficult for the listener to find the point of the story. She didn't tell me why Johnny was shot. It became clearer that Alice saw herself more as a historian than a teller of tales. The local historian and storyteller have different goals, which accounts for the difference in the focus of their styles and lack of evaluative comments. Like Gay Robie, Alice was very anxious for me to realize that she was telling me accurate, true stories. Del's audiences didn't care whether his stories were true or not, according to Mary Auvil and other family members.

Alice volunteered the next story after Ron had finished a funny anecdote. She was probably telling a third-person anecdote known well in the community since there was no indication she witnessed the event.

"The Ottos"
Alice Mahurin, 1985

The Ottos,
they lived on the road on the way to Bows and Joseph.
Old Otto was crossing the White Bird bridge
and it went down.

Somebody asked him one time—
what in the world they were going to do
    about the White Bird bridge?
He said,
"I don't know."

He'd already done his part.

"We got it down."

Cattle drive through White Bird
Photo courtesy Grangeville Bicentennial Museum

Actually, this story resembled a joke. Its short, snappy form convinced me that she had related this story before. I thought it could be one of her son's stories. She definitely wanted to be in on the joke-like session as she began this right after Ron told of a practical joke he had played on the Jewetts. Again her story partook of the local attitude that antics of local characters make a good source of entertainment. She obviously enjoyed telling the story, and had a good chuckle out of it.

While Alice and Gay Robie obviously could hold their own in story-swapping sessions with men, unlike them, the women's stories contained no profanity. Alice relished telling a good story in a ladylike way. When her son Ron used ample doses of rough language during our conversation in her presence, she didn't flinch. It just wasn't part of her style to use it. I suspect this tendency reflects a larger cultural style pattern. Women of Alice's age and period apparently did not normally include such expressions in their storytelling.

Alice Mahurin had her own unique presentation style, a muffled monotone. Her literary framing without dialogue, and just little indirect hints of it now and then, was quite unique to her. The folkloric feature that strongly linked her with tradition was the fact that as a teller of local character stories, she portrayed many of the same characters others chose. The Mrs. Benedict, Jewett, and Nevins stories all contain the same characters that Del Ringer used. It was obvious as well that this was not the first time this mother and son had spent an evening together telling stories for others of the old days. Telling stories of their shared past seemed a significant pastime for them.

Chapter Ten Notes

[1] According to information provided by Ron Mahurin on page 243 in *Idaho Voices,* his house is thought to be the oldest house in the county. It was built by a ship's carpenter for John Wood in 1862. The lumber was reportedly sawed up river at John Day and floated down in the form of a raft. Martha Ringer remembered the house when the Tiptons lived there. Alice Mahurin and her husband Walter lived in the house with their son Ron until their deaths. Alice died in 1985, not long after our interview. In 1986, Ron married Ruth Brogan and they now live in the old house.

[2] See pages 260–261 in *Idaho County Voices* for the life stories of Edward and Isabella Robie. While Del spoke of him as the Irishman, his family had been in the United States for a long time having come as Pilgrims on the Mayflower.

[3] See pages 236–237 in *Idaho Voices* for an account of the lives of Sam and Mary Large. Both were born in Ireland. They are buried in the Slate Creek Cemetery.

[4] Ron contributed a section on his parents' history for *Idaho Voices*, pp. 242–3.

[5] Alice wrote me a letter dated September 16, 1985, in which she said this picture appeared in an article, "War of 1877: Centennial of Sorrow" in the *Lewiston Morning Tribune.* I assumed it must have been in 1977, the centennial of the war. She did not know the article date. She wrote in her letter: "I read the part under the picture and it read, 'Wounded Head, a Nez Perce warrior, took Mrs. Benedict on his horse and took her back to Salmon River where they shook hands and parted, and where she then worked her way back to Camas Prairie.'" Alice added that she was surprised, saying, "I always thought Aunt Frankie Benedict Shissler told me she never told on him or he would have been killed by the Indians, but it could have been he told later."

[6] See Alfreda Elsensohn, *Pioneer Days in Idaho County,* 272, for yet another telling of Mrs. Benedict's story. The account given here appears closer to Alice Mahurin's version than Del Ringer's.

[7] See Bailey, *The River of No Return,* 258–260, for several accounts of the fate of Mrs. John L. Manuals. While there is no mention of her getting her tongue cut out by the Indians, it states she was captured by the Indians and was supposedly murdered by them.

[8] When I visited Ron Mahurin in 1994, he gave me an account of the Indian War to read. He said this pamphlet had been in his family's possession for a long time. It was titled "The Nez Perce Indian War under War Chiefs Joseph and White Bird," by Charlotte M. Kirkwood, printed by the Idaho Country Free Press, Grangeville, Idaho, by special permission of the Mrs. Lenore Kirkwood Rogers, daughter of the author. There was no date on it. Mrs. Kirkwood, Sr. came to visit a son in Grangeville in 1890 and collected accounts of the war from survivors. She didn't type it up until she was eighty, and her daughter had it published "sometime after World War II." On page 49 begins "the thrilling account of Mrs. Benedict's Escape to Mt. Idaho with her Children." According to this account, the Indians killed Mr. Benedict because he did not help bring to justice Larry Ott who had killed an old blind Indian. Mrs. Kirkwood quotes Mrs. Benedict as saying that when the Indians approached her cabin her husband told her to take the children and fly. Mrs. Benedict said, "No, I won't leave you." He replied, "Think of the children." Mrs. Kirkwood wrote that Mrs. Benedict then set out for Mount Idaho taking a little money and a few trinkets among which was a gold cross of which Joseph robbed her before releasing her. Mrs. Benedict told Mrs. Kirkwood that she traveled by night and reached the home of a Mrs. Manuel, who "showed me her knees and what the Indians had done to them," but would not come with her. Then Mrs. Benedict related to Mrs. Kirkwood how she hid near the White Bird grade and heard the Indians "passing all night and dare not move." The next morning Mrs. Benedict met soldiers fleeing from the battle and saw "many rider less horse with turned saddles." (Evidently the soldiers had loosened the girths on the saddles to rest the horse just before the surprise attack.) Some of the soldiers helped her to get further away.

After they left her off, she was captured by the Indians who put her behind on a horse. Finally, she met some squaws who compelled them "to set me down." Soon thereafter, Mrs. Benedict said, "Imagine my surprise when I realized that it was a friend coming to my rescue, Mr. Robie, who had gone out to look for me." He took her to safety at Mount Idaho. Mrs. Kirkwood's version of Mrs. Benedict's story resembles that of Alice Mahurin more than that of Del Ringer.

[9] Sandra K. Dolby-Stahl, "A Literary Folklorist Methodology for the Study of Meaning in Personal Narrative," *Journal of Folklore Research*, Vol. 22, No. 1 (April 1985), p. 62.

[10] The collapse of the bridge as Otto crossed occurred the morning of August 11, 1932, according to Johnny Carrey and Cort Conley in *The River of No Return*, p. 287.

Chapter Eleven:
Ron Mahurin

I got the ladder out of Old Pough's store. Old lady Pough couldn't see, so she used a flashlight to find dress materials and stuff you know. And I got an old safe, and it's got Salmon River State Bank written on it. Went out of business in 1920s.

—Ron Mahurin, 1985

Pough's Store
Photo Courtesy Grangeville Bicentennial Museum

While Ron Mahurin (who described himself as "a crazy kind of a bastard") was only thirty-nine at the time of the September 1, 1985 interview, I found him to be a gold mine of information about local history, lore, and characters. He took us to the sites of the Ringer and Harrah homesteads to visit local cemeteries and to the 1877 Indian War battle area. Ron proved to be a font of all kinds of folk wisdom. For example, he showed us how to find ticks in hackberry seeds saying, "People that are smart with education tell me I'm crazier than hell, but if that ain't a tick. See them little legs. See them wiggle."

Ron Mahurin explains ticks are found in hackberry seeds
Photo MHB 1985

As cemetery commissioner, Ron knows the location of every grave in the region, and the story of each person buried there. Ron led us to a tiny isolated graveyard on a hill high above the Salmon where he pointed out graves with such markers as, "Harry Mason, Plucked from his family by the rude hands of savages."[1] He said, "I'm sure there are more graves up here 'cause it's so flat. It so hilly, any big old flat rock could be a grave stone." When we returned to the cemetery in 1994, we found it now had a marker designating the "French cemetery" with graves dated 1877 of William Osborn and Harry Mason.

William Osborne stone
Photo MHB 1985

Ron Mahurin and Paul Bennett, author
Photo MHB1985

When we visited the scene of the White Bird Hill Indian battle, Ron's account, he claimed, was more accurate and complete than the official narrative that appears on the roadside historical marker. As we looked at the scene he made remarks like, "See Howard camped up there on that ridge. All that ridge where it was flat, that's where Howard camped, up there on the skyline."

Nez Perce battle site near White Bird
Photo MHB 1985

I was hoping Ron might have heard of some of the characters that Del Ringer storied about, and I was not disappointed. I had found the right person. He relished telling us this story about the Jewetts.

"Log Pull at the Jewett's"
Ron Mahurin, 1985

See, the Jewetts had a house,
    and it burnt.
Then Old Bill moved
    into the old house again.

We was up there,
    Ronnie Johnson and I.

I was the one what done it.
I set the dogs on,
     the sons of bitches.

The old cow went over the bank,
     and under the road,
     and through the fence,
     and he had the fence
     tied to an old log in the house.

When that damned old cow went
     through the fence
why it pulled the log out of the house,
     and we had to help Old Bill
          pry up the house,
     and put the log back in the house.
He was madder than hell at us.
He gathered his old horse up,
     and went to get it.

When I heard this tale I knew this was unquestionably a story in the same tradition as Del Ringer's Jewett stories. It appeared Ron Mahurin was from the same mold as Del. Amazingly, this story was being told by someone almost half a century younger than Del Ringer. I could imagine Del pulling this prank.

Ron used "old" as a modifier, as Del had. He used some profanity, which Del was not averse to using. Unlike Del, Ron used no dialogue, but like Del, Ron's style was sparse. There was the minimum detail and description for the story to make sense. There was some irony because Old Bill was not aware of what was going on. It was definitely a story with Del's brand of humor, using no elaborate literary features, only the common simile, "madder than hell." After Ron finished his story about Bill Jewett, Alice added this comment, "Old Bill, he just couldn't help himself," a judgment on his simplicity. Then Alice followed Ron's story with a comment to complete it, suggesting to me that she has a version of this story:

Then Jewett sat here
and watched his house burn down
and said,
    prettiest sight he ever saw.
    "Prettiest sight I ever did see."

At this point Alice told the story about Otto, who collapsed the bridge at White Bird in a cattle drive. There was a story-swapping session between mother and son going on. While Ron told personal experience stories, he also enjoyed passing on a good humorous story from the old days "before his time," like this one he told next about one of Old Man Wyatt's hands.

"Old Man Wyatt's Cows" (1)
Ron Mahurin, 1985
Old Wyatt.
I think it was during the Depression.
See
they couldn't get nothin' for the cows,
and they didn't have no money.
And a cold hard winter here,
and they had 'em right down on the river there,
and they had a guy in a tarpaper shack there,
    some where at the mouth of Deer Creek,
and Old Wyatt was in town here,
and I guess he was drunk,
and had been for a week.
A few days anyhow.

So anyway he come and asked Old Wyatt
    what to do about it.
Said he couldn't stand to look out at it.
Every time he looked
    there was one of them cows
a-slidin' off the hill!
Old Wyatt told him,
    well,
    then he better look out the other window!

I was delighted to find another story about Old Man Wyatt and his hands. I can just imagine Del's telling this story, or at least enjoying it. Of course, I am sure Del would have told the story in dialogue, but Ron, like Alice, preferred indirect discourse as in the line, "so anyway he come and asked Old Wyatt what to do about it." Similar to his mom's style, there was rhythm with the repetition of the word "and." Like the other tellers Ron used a simple vocabulary of common words and colloquial forms, like "a-slidin'" and "old." His stance was that of a not-so-objective narrator, as he obviously wasn't a witness, saying, "I think it was during the Depression." He was telling a story handed down to him.

This story was close to a joke format. It didn't have an evaluative statement with the point like most stories include, but rather consisted of a complication and punch line. Ron introduced it by saying, "The only one I ever heard about Wyatt was this one," a remark which indicates that he had heard a number of such joke-like stories. His comment added evidence that he was operating out of an oral tradition of such stories.

Ron Mahurin at the old homestead
Photo MHB 1994

Ron was a much more animated storyteller than his mother or Del, perhaps because of his youth. He used considerable vocal variation, animated facial expressions, and large gestures and movements. He was obviously an accomplished storyteller, but he deferred to his mother throughout most of our interview in 1985. He gave us a second version of "Old Man Wyatt's Cows" later that night when we ran into him at the tavern in White Bird. This version shows the effect of the tavern context, since Ron felt freer to use profanity there.

"Old Man Wyatt's Cows" (2)

Old Man Wyatt had a lot of cows
    over on Leery Mountain.
They was all a-rollin'
They had somebody livin'
    in an old tarpaper shack and
Old Man Wyatt was in town drunk.

It was all froze up, and
    the damn cows was rollin' off the mountain.

So the fellow went in to White Bird and
    asked Old Wyatt what to do.
Said
    every time he looked out the goddamn window
    saw a goddamn cow rollin' by.

Old Man Wyatt told him
    to look out the other goddamn window!

In May 1994, I made a brief visit to Slate Creek and spent a pleasant evening chatting with Ron and his wife Ruth. He again proved to be a gracious host. When the subject of Old Man Wyatt came up, he repeated the story "Old Man Wyatt's Cows." The third version followed closely those I had previously recorded, and he felt free to use the profanity. Again we spent time talking about the history of the region, and the various folks whose graves lie in the cemeteries for which Ron has voluntarily assumed care. In many cases, all the relatives are gone. Ron receives no compensation for his efforts. He takes pride in knowing the story of the graves. He cares for their upkeep to make sure there is a visual, as well as oral, memory of these Salmon River pioneers.

Ron Mahurin, guardian of old cemeteries
Photo MHB 1995

The feature that really links Ron with Del Ringer in a common tradition is that he told ironic local character anecdotes about the same characters Del did: the Jewetts and Old Man Wyatt. That both he and his mother chose to tell the same type of story about the same characters in a similar style, convinced me that they were acting out of a common storytelling tradition from this area of the Salmon River. It was gratifying to learn that this tradition had not died out with Del Ringer, and those of his generation, and that younger folks like Ron Mahurin, are carrying on.

Chapter Twelve:
Gus Carlson

I was up at the C. C. camp one time. They was a-buildin'
the road up here, the C. C.'s got up there, at what we
call the big rock, and I was talkin' to the foreman. Here
come a CC, didn't have no clothes on, packin' a box of
dynamite on his shoulders. Boss said, "What's the hell
the idea of packing that with no clothes on?" "Well," he
said, "you work me like a horse, I got to act like one."

—Gus Carlson, September 1985

Gay Robie had intrigued me with her stories about John Kimbrough
in 1984. I was pleased to learn that his nephew, Gus Carlson, lived
nearby. Gus and his family were owners of the last of the sheep outfits in
this region. Their lands extended some fifty miles up the river. Earlier,
Delbert Wicks had described Gus as "the big frog in this pond," and
with Gay's description of him as "the biggest duck in the puddle around
here now," I felt some apprehension that he might not be receptive to
meeting with me. However, my fears were ungrounded as he accepted
my request for an interview and gave me a marvelous two hours of
stories. Gus turned out to be a very lively storyteller.

I found Gus and his wife Opal in a large log home surrounded
by well-irrigated gardens. Opal Patterson Carlson has a reputation as
a talented painter of western art scenes. I saw her paintings exhibited

at the Labor Day weekend art show in Riggins. Both Opal and Gus
came from pioneer families. Opal's family was the Irwins. Her great-
grandfather, Isaac Irwin, bought the flat around the present site of
Riggins for a horse and a watch.[1] Her father was a farmer up on White
Bird Ridge. Opal, telling of the family tradition of storytelling, said:

> I wish you could have met my mother's uncle, Dick
> Irwin. I wish I'd have been more interested then. He
> loved to tell stories. He told stories about life before
> there was even a road through here. Some people
> starved trying to get from north to south through this
> river area. He told me stories about people trying to get
> through here with ox carts, and how they would get
> tangled up with bluffs they couldn't get around. He
> told me about this one family that was trying to get
> to New Meadows, and they couldn't get around the
> bluffs, and winter come on. They had to eat their oxen,
> and carry what little they could. His father would tell
> those stories, my grandfather.[2]

Gus's father immigrated to "I-dee-ho," as Gus called it, from
Sweden, along with a sister and brother. His mother's family came
by covered wagon and "landed down out of Midvale in Crane Creek
where they took up a homestead." John Kimbrough was his mother's
brother. Gus had been in the sheep business since the age of seventeen,
starting out as a herder and ending up owning a big sheep outfit. Gus
said, "We are the only ones left in the sheep business." He and Opal
had been married fifty-three years when I interviewed them in 1985.
Their son Mick had taken over running the ranch.

Gus described himself as a hard worker who did not go in for
fancy clothes, airs, or drinking. He said:

> I remember one time after a wool growers' meeting, I
> went in a store where they sold sodi pop. I wasn't married
> then. I had on my overalls, and I went in there, and all
> the rest of them was dressed up. They were giving me

a hard time. Thought I could wear better clothes on account of I wasn't married and didn't have no expenses. So I told 'em I was the only one here that represents the business as it really is. Times was hard. We was selling lambs for eight cents a pound, and wool for five.

I took a photograph of him as he showed me a coffee tin he packed for years sheepherding. He said:

I've got an old coffee can that's got NRA on it. I used it in the sheep camp. The lid goes back on it just like it did first time I took it off. The herders used to smoke Bull Durham. I put matches in there. That can is just as good as the day when I bought it.

Gus Carlson holding an old tin he packed for sheepherding
Photo MHB

Gus put his life out there as a sheep man, treated his help well, and, as you will see in his stories, was very loyal to them. He said, "We lived real good in sheep camp all the time. I asked my men what they wanted to eat, and that's what I brought out." During the Depression, when other outfits only paid thirty dollars a month, Gus paid forty. He said:

> I didn't have tin plates, and we had a tablecloth. That was our home out there and we had a clean camp. We had good stuff and furnished good, and I paid my men good too. And if they took a vacation I never docked 'em. I've got mad enough to kill 'em but I never docked 'em. One spring I was gatherin' a bunch of sheep up here on Berg Mountain before lambin' them, and the herder came to town and got drunk, and I gathered them sheep all by myself, and didn't have no dog worth nothin', and that night I saw him a-comin' across the river and I said, "I hope you drown!" When they are sober they are great though.

Gus defended his herders even though their antics often frustrated him. He said, "You know some folks say, sheepherders are the dumbest people in the world, but I've learned some things from those people that I couldn't learn from a feller that supposed to be smart." To this Opal added this humorous remark: "Well, you know, they have a saying and the cowboys turn it around—a sheepherder is a cowboy with his brains knocked out." I had no doubts that I was on to another good storyteller. I thought it interesting that Gus described the sort of stories I'd been hearing as "windy stories." In my opinion, he used "windy" to mean a lively story about the old days, a good tale told engagingly so it holds the listener's attention. It did not mean one that is necessarily untrue or true. Gus's windy stories were mostly personal experience narratives about his life as a sheepherder and running the ranch, and about the funny and serious episodes of characters he experienced along the way.[3] Like Del's stories of horse swapping, Gus told a swapping tale.[4] His was about swapping sheep dogs. His favorite dog was an old half-breed his son brought home that was "a dog you just couldn't lose sheep with." The fellow in this story was not so fortunate.

"The Dog That Came Down Center"[5]
Gus Carlson, 1985

I come into McCall one time.
    There was a sheepherder.
They used to tell big windy stories, you know.
Feller asked him,
    "What kind of a dog you got there?"

    "I got the best dog in the world.
    Do anything you like."
All he would do was
    just go half around a band of sheep,
    and come down through the center.
That's the worse thing in the world, you know.

So they sent his dog out,
    and he got around there,
    "Come down through the center!"
    "Come down through the center!"
    and he come down through,
    and the feller bought the dog.
    The only thing it would do!

Them sheepherders used to tell some awful windy stories.
I wish I had wrote down
    the sayings of these old-timers.
They'd tell stories,
    come to town and get drunk,
and gosh
    they were something!

In "The Dog That Came Down Center," Gus's vocabulary, not surprisingly, like that of the other narrators, was simple without abstract or sophisticated usage. Like Delbert Wicks he used "them" as a modifier for "those." He used "gosh" as filler, and "you know," as Del did. The colloquial "feller" took the place of "fellow" in most of his conversation and stories.

The characteristic lack of literary devices such as metaphors and similes that I had noted in other Salmon River narrators was apparent here as well. The descriptive detail in this story was sparse. He used repetition for effect in, *"Come down through the center!"* A great similarity to Del Ringer lay in Gus's use of irony. Everyone including the listeners knew that coming down the center was all the dog could do, except of course the poor buyer who ought to have been aware. Gus's mock-serious rendition of yelling, *"Come down through the center!"* was very funny. His dramatized dialogue in this story was the highlight.

One story flowed without interruption to another. Opal occasionally made a remark simultaneously, but Gus would continue and she would defer to him. I had asked Gus to tell me about his uncle, John Kimbrough, whom Gay Robie had talked about. Gus continued with the following story:

"John Kimbrough Gets Hired"
Gus Carlson, 1985

My uncle that come in this country,
he was a banker for the sheepherders.
He was a bachelor.
I remember him.
He had all gold teeth,
    and chewed tobacco,
    and drank whiskey.

Scott Bundage was runnin' sheep
    and he needed a sheepherder.[6]
So John was a-ploughin' when Scott come by.
He just unhitched the horses,
    and turned 'em loose.
Left the harness there at the plough,
    and went off with him to keep sheep.

My grandfather got on his horse the next day,
    and went over and told Scott,

"Don't hire that kid.
He's not worth a damn for nothin'!
He won't work or nothin' else!"

The next thing you know my uncle bought the
   man out in the sheep business.
He carried these people
   here in this country in the early days.
I got backin' from him too into the sheep business.

This story immediately reminded me of Del Ringer's tale about Henry Ricke, who planted walnuts in spite of the belief of his friends and neighbors that it was a ridiculous action, and that Henry was an awkward simpleton because of his ill-fitting clothes. Here we have a kid who was "not worth a damn for nothin'," becoming the most powerful man in the region.

Since Gus would have been too young, or not even born, when the incident took place, he must have been relating a story that was handed down in his family or in the region. Gus was, however, a witness of the material used in the opening and close of the story. His lines of dialogue were the climax of the story. While Gus gave little descriptive detail, the lines about his Uncle's gold teeth, chewing tobacco, and drinking whiskey characterized John. There was some irony since, unlike the grandfather and Scott Bundage, we listeners, and of course the narrator, knew that John Kimbrough became a very prominent man.

Gus continued after finishing the story with this further assessment of his uncle in answer to my question, "What was his personality like?"

He was a man that if you were a workin' man, he'd visit
with you. If you come with fine clothes, all dressed up,
he wouldn't care for that. He was a honest man. He
wouldn't say anything that would hurt anybody, and
his word was as good as gold. He was a bachelor, and
kind of an odd fellow. He started in the sheep business
and made a go of it when many went bust.

Gus followed next with a story in response to Opal's prompting, "Tell her about the deef fellows." I took that as a clue that it was a repeated story in his repertoire.

"The Deef Fellows"[7]
Gus Carlson, 1985

Well, there was Ace Maily.
He liked to trade with someone
    and get the best of him.
So Ace Maily saw this feller, and told him
that when they was goin' to meet to swap horses,
    "You better talk loud, he's awful deef."
And he told the other feller the same thing,
    "You better talk loud, he's awful deef."
So there they both were
    standin' up there
    yellin' at each other,
    and folks a-wonderin'
    if there was somethin' the matter with 'em!

Gus continued to use regional speech patterns in this story. Martha Ringer and Gay Robie also pronounced "deaf" as "deef." He used "a-wonderin'," a verb form that Del and the other narrators used frequently. Like Gay Robie he used "awful" to mean "very." Gus again used repetition in the two lines: "You better talk loud, he's awful deef." He gave this story a lively presentation with a sense of urgency communicated about the necessity to "talk loud" which, of course, Gus did as he said the lines. Here was another ironical story in which we know something the characters didn't. It was a similar trick to the one Del played on the Berlinghoff boys when he and Clay Davis moved the gates. Gus gave no attributions for this story. In fact, I found it is an example of a widely circulated tale type that has been indexed. Opal knew it as well.[8]

Gus flowed from this story into one memory after another. Next he described the old Fourth of July celebrations when they used to bet on "piss ants." The crowd would draw a circle around the ants and place bets on where the ants would crawl out. Gus said he started with a dollar and ended up with over six hundred dollars one Fourth. Then he said they played baseball games at which no one could bat until all the bets were placed. He followed next with "The Madame at Burgdorf," a rich personal experience story filled with vivid scenes. It was a multiple-episode story that tells of a journey he made in the middle of winter as a teenager on his first trip away from home. It must have been an important memory for him, for he repeated many times, "I never will forget it."

"The Madame at Burgdorf"[9]
Gus Carlson, 1985

I never will forget
    when I first went in there.
When I first went in there at Burgdorf.

They had a tunnel from one house to another.
    And old man Burgdorf
    had the hot springs that was named after him.
    (That's out of McCall about thirty-two miles.)

And this lady come in from Canada,
    and she was a madame
    and they got married
    and had a two story hotel.

I never will forget it
    as long as I live.

We was in a toboggan.
    It was about ten, twelve, maybe fourteen feet long,
    and four feet wide, maybe wider.

And we had two big horses,
    weigh maybe fifteen hundred pounds.
    Had one in front of the other.
    Had snow shoes on,
    didn't drive 'em.

They'd just go,
    "clompedy, clomp."

The trail was broke,
    and if they stepped off a little,
they'd get right back on.

The snow was thirty-two feet deep.
You could see marks on the signal trees.
They used to have lots of snow.
It took three days to get from McCall to Warren.

The first day you went half way
and stayed there.
The next day to Burgdorf,
    and you stayed there all night.
I was going in there
    to a sheepherding job on the south fork.
I had never been away from home in my whole life.

Well, we got to Halfway,
    and them old-timers was makin' me feel bad,
    tellin' me all what I had to go through.

I was just a green kid,
    havin' never been out before.
I never will forget it.

We got there at Halfway,
    and an old storyteller,
Motts was his name,
    and just full of stories you know,
    and he was a-tellin' about
        trailin' a bear all day.
I was a-listenin' to him
    tell it to a couple of fellers there,
        and they were kind of green,
and one of them says,
    "Why didn't you shoot him?"
He said,
    "Why shoot uphill,
    and strain the barrel of my gun.
    Hell, no!"

So we got in there to Burgdorf,
    and said that she was awful ornery you know.

I was just a kid, and half scared to death,
    and I only had a dollar and fifteen cents.
I didn't have enough to pay for my lodgings—
    at least I didn't think I had enough.

She was settin' in a chair by the window,
and he sittin' on her lap.
I never will forget that.

So when we got in there,
    I hunted her up
and I said,
(Well, my uncle had this outfit over on the river,
    but I didn't want to tell 'em
    I was any relation to him.
    I didn't want to belittle him.)
So I told her I didn't have any money,
    but that I had a job, and
    that when I got the money I'd pay her.

    "Well," she said, "we'll see kid."
Just like that.

So I said if there was anything I could do
        I'd be willing to do that.
    "No," she said.

I ate with the cooks.
There was three women.

Then when I got ready to go to bed,
she said,
    "Follow me kid."
And we went out through a tunnel in the snow to their cabin.
and I slept in their bed,
    and it had feather ticks on the bed,
and her jewelry was just a-settin' there,
and hand made furniture made out
    of that knotty pine, knots all over it,
and some feller had peeled them knots,

and made furniture out of it.
And that was her room,
and that's where I spent the night.

Next morning when I got ready to go,
Said,
    "Mrs. Burgdorf,
    what do I owe you
        so I can send it on to you?"
I had a dollar and fifteen cents.

She said,
    "You owe me a dollar and fifteen cents."

"Well, I got a dollar and fifteen cents."
(To this day I don't know how she knew
        I had a dollar and fifteen cents.)
I paid her.
    Give her the dollar and fifteen cents.
I got supper, breakfast, and bed, and
she packed me a lunch for
a dollar and fifteen cents!

Horses on snowshoes
Photo courtesy Grangeville Bicentennial Museum

After hearing this story, I knew I had found a teller the equal of Del Ringer. Del would have liked the irony and humor in the incident about telling the greenhorns that you shouldn't shoot a rifle uphill or you'd strain the barrel. Here once more was the attitude that it's ok to poke fun at greenhorns. In this story, Gus himself was the greenhorn, and he was enjoying his own naiveté in retrospect as well.

Gus styled this story in his own delightful way. While the story was mostly told in the past tense, he did use present for past tense at times, like Alice Mahurin. While the dialogue was very limited, it was vivid and brought the story to life wherever it appeared. Gus used a wealth of description, as in the scene on the trail of breaking the way for the horses on snow shoes with statistics about depth of snow, size of horse, etc., that added authenticity. He even used a sound effect, "clompedy, clomp." He again used repetition returning to the line, "I never will forget it," four times, and the line, "dollar and fifteen cents," six times. The climax came in his surprise statement at the coincidence of Mrs. Burgdorf's charging just exactly the amount he had, a dollar and fifteen cents. Similar to Gay Robie's style, the constant repetition of "and" gave the story a melodic quality as he performed it.

Gus gave a dramatic performance of this story, with full character voices for the Madame and Old Motts. He had a sense of pacing, building each episode to a climax then dropping his voice and level of energy as he began the next one. The overall effect was that of an energetic, fast-paced story. By the time he performed this story, and the one before it about the Fourth of July, his son's wife and children had quietly slipped in and Gus had a large and most appreciative family audience. This did not appear to be an unusual occasion for them, adding to my contention that the tradition of family stories was alive and well along the Salmon River at the time of my visit.

Next, Gus began talking about a fellow named John Phelan. I knew I had heard of John Phelan before; then I realized he was the same herder who had left Gay Robie and her brother Johnny when I heard their childhood story of the encounter with a bear. Gus related one of his childhood memories of John:

We used to have a lot of poker games in the Monte
Carlo saloon here. John Phelan always packed a six-
shooter. He was sittin' there playin' poker with a gallon
jug of moonshine sittin' between his legs. I was down
at the dance, heard the internal revenue guys were
a-comin', so I beat it up there and asked John to give
me the jug and hid it for him. I was just a kid, but I was
the only one he would listen to.

Monte Carlo Saloon
Photo Grangeville Bicentennial Museum

In "John Phelan Goes to Walla Walla," Gus merged two stories
together. When I first heard the second one, I thought a sheriff had
trailed John Phelan up the mountain at night because of a murder in
the first story. It was actually a sheriff and internal revenue men who
were after John for moonshining. It was easy to detect Gus's attitude
about the murder, by the way. The line, "nobody liked him," indicated
that Gus felt the fellow got what he deserved. Gus, however, approved
of John Phelan, "an awful good herder."

"John Phelan Goes to Walla Walla"
Gus Carlson 1985

John Phelan was an awful good herder,
He killed a man.
He said
that was the longest hour in his whole life
    when the jury was out.
They come back and turned him loose.

How it was.
They went to a dance,
    and a bully in that country
a big ranch boy jumped on a fellow
    and got him down.
John told him,
    "He can't whip you.
    He's not man enough to do it."

    "Well, maybe you want some of it."

    "No, I'm not a fightin' man."
He got John down,
    and John cut him clear open,
He said,
    said it was the hardest cuttin' he ever did.
And they left that fellow a-layin' there
    from one o'clock in the morning,
    until three o'clock in the afternoon.
Nobody liked him.

John was an awful good sheepherder.

John, he moonshined,
    and the sheriff decided to come after him.

He run to a widow lady there.
He said,
    "Where'll I hide?"

She said to him,
    "Hide behind the trunk."

So he got behind the trunk,
    and she threw some big old blankets over him.

The internal revenue men come in.
    "You seen anything of John Phelan?"

    No, they hadn't.
He was under the quilts,
    just about choking to death
    waiting for them to leave.

He come back to this country,
    up Preacher Road.

I was just a kid tending camp.
They had him camped up on this mountain here.
When I come down with the pack string,
    the internal revenuers and the sheriff was going up.
They wanted to know where John's camp was,
    and I wouldn't tell 'em.
They followed the mule string up there.

I unpacked my mules
    and climbed that mountain that night.
And I got up there
    and the sheep was bedded
        on a little flat like that,
    and there was a little rise
    and then that big flat.
One officer was on one side,
    and one over on the other.
It was a moonlight night,
    and I was maybe fifty feet from the tent,
    and I'd throw rocks at the tent,
    and the dog would bark,
    but John would get after the dog, you know.
He couldn't figure out what it was.

Well, I was up there the next morning.
I didn't know whether they'd shoot me
   or anything!

I told John
   "I tried to warn you."

"Oh," he said,
   "I could have got away
   by running over the hill."

He had pyorrhea on one side of his face
   on account of his teeth,
and he said to the law enforcement officers
   that he would like to have a drink.

So they went down there by the creek
   and took about that much in a quart bottle,
   and he drank that whiskey
   until they got up there to New Meadows.

When they got to New Meadows,
   why they was going to have something to eat,
   and they was going down the sidewalk
      one on one side, and one on the other,
   had him handcuffed to one guy
      taking him back to Oregon.

   "Where to?
   "Where to?"

John, he jerked the sheriff by the handcuff,
and said,

   "I'm takin'
   the son of a bitch to Walla Walla!"

Gus told this story in a series of dramatic episodes. The descriptive material and details were used to build up to the exciting moments of dramatized scene. Gus ended the story with another example of the

Salmon River ironic humor, when John indicates to the "passerby" that he is taking the sheriff to Walla Walla, and, of course, we knew it was the other way around.

As Gus told this story, he derived obvious enjoyment. He was laughing until the tears ran down his cheeks as he told about John's hiding under the quilts, or jerking the sheriff's arm. His telling style was a contrast to Del's restrained, dry, quiet presentations. Gus used many gestures which gave an impression of tremendous vitality as he storied rapidly and forcefully. Here was an excellent example of two very different individual presentational styles within the broader cultural tradition.

Opal mentioned that she too had heard many windy stories, and that John Phelan was the subject of a good many tales she had heard. She said John was from Tennessee and that he always pronounced "ewes" as "yous." When Gus finished his story about John, Opal added this ending:

> John in his latter years when he got trouble in his hips, he got married and he and his wife settled here in Riggins. Raised chickens, and sold eggs in Riggins. He died right here.

Gus talked of how reckless John and other herders were with their earnings. Gus told of John Phelan's losing everything gambling after working tremendously hard for the money. That story ends:

> So I took him in the restaurant in New Meadows
> after workin' hard at mouthin' the sheep,
>   and he got in a poker game,
>   and lost seven hundred dollars that night
>   and the next day he went back to work.

A herder named Charlie French left camp with eighteen hundred dollars to get new teeth, and came back with no teeth or money. Another took his large sum of money to a dance and remarked to his partner, "I'm kind of afraid with all this money." His partner said, "Here give it to me," and obligingly put it in her bosom. Gus said, "I tried hard to get them to save their money. I did everything. I hated to see them work and throw their money away. It bothered me awful bad." He said one fellow, Bill Borden, went out for a break from herding and he didn't see him again for forty years. I enjoyed Gus's colorful description of John's moonshining activities. Gus said John offered to share his products with him, but since Gus was not a drinking man, he gave his share to his uncle, John Kimbrough. Gus said of the moonshiners:

> They always put it in a five gallon charred oak keg, 110 proof.
> And when they poured in there,
> it looked just like water.
> And when they took it out,
> it looked just like karo syrup.
> It was a beautiful color.
> I never did drink any of it.
> My uncle he'd have a toddy about twice a day.
>
> One of the local moonshining operations was in a dairy,
> And they was shipping out whiskey in cream cans.
> They stored the whiskey where the cows stood in the barn.

Gus and Del Ringer shared some similar attitudes and characters in their stories. I asked Gus if he knew the Jewetts. Gus replied by telling a story about Old Lady Jewett helping herself to items in his supply store thinking she was unobserved. Gus just picked up the items in question on her way out the door, and rung them up as though nothing had happened. Neither of them ever mentioned the incident. Gus said of her, "You ought to have known Old Lady Jewett," to which Opal added, "Boy, was she a character. They were quite an outfit." Incidentally, here we see two local words that Del Ringer liked, "old" and "outfit." Gus defended the Jewetts. He respected their grit and perseverance. Said Gus, "Well, I'll tell you, they may have been simple but were a lot smarter than you'd think they were. They got by. A lot of people went broke and they still existed."

Del Ringer shared this admiration for the Jewetts' grit and the fact that they kept going. In 1975, Del told me this incident about Old Man Jewett.[9]

Old man Jewett had rheumatism awful bad. I come there one time he was a-ploughin' in the spring. It was wet and the ground was cold and wet. He'd go a ways. He had it in his legs so bad, he'd lay down in that farrow back of that plough. I seen him for maybe a quarter of a mile lyin' back there, before I got to him. I thought the old man must have died. Seen him lyin' behind the plough. He was very much alive, but his rheumatism was a-botherin' him. That old guy was tough. Nothin' stop him.

Gus, like Del Ringer, respected and liked the Nez Perce Indians. Gus said, "Them old time Indians was good people." When an old squaw complained to Gus that the Indians were having a hard time with the game warden about their killing and eating game, Gus advised her, "Just say, 'No savvy,' when they come by and ask you a lot of questions." Gus said, "Next time I stopped to see her she said it had worked just fine."

Another attitude he shared with Del Ringer was that it was important to maintain order and to exhibit good behavior at dances. However, Gus added, referring to the dance hall fights, "It was just good fun." The last story Gus told me was about the makeshift jail Charlie Clay set up at dances. After Charlie retired from the sheep business, he became deputy sheriff. Charlie would arrest fellows who became rowdy at dances at the schoolhouse in Riggins and "put 'em in jail." Gus described a typical dance as follows:

"Charlie Clay's Jail"
Gus Carlson, 1985

Charlie Clay,
his jail was out in front of the dance hall.
They had a lot of little quaking Aspen trees,
    four to six inches around.
So he'd just put handcuffs on 'em,
    and handcuff 'em to a tree.
    and they'd set there,
    and they'd cry.

You'd go by
  and there would be four or five of them
    handcuffed to the trees.
Hell, it was a lot of fun in those days.
There ain't fun like that anymore.
It was all clean fun.

The revenue officer would come in,
and boy, they'd be a-goin' this way and that
    hidin' their liquor you know.
Sometimes they'd be dancin' away in there,
  and somebody would holler, "Fight,"
  and everybody would be outside.
Then they'd go back in
  and dance some more.

We had a lot of fun then.

Gus Carlson and Del Ringer seemed cut from the same cloth. Both exhibited great mastery in dialogue. They peppered their speech with colorful local words like "a-goin'" and "boy." They were masters at creating succinct descriptive details and using repetition. Both were nonstop tellers whose stories flowed one into another without any coaxing. Both told animal-swapping stories. They enjoyed poking fun at local characters and unsuspecting greenhorns, but were proud of hardworking fellows like Henry Ricke the walnut planter and John Kimbrough the "walking bank." Gus alluded to a long tradition of windy stories in his background. Like Del, he assimilated this tradition well. Old Motts had nothing on either of them when it came to telling windy stories. When I visited Ron Mahurin in 1999, he told me that Gus had passed on.

Chapter Twelve Notes

[1] See "Isaac and Noah Irwin Families" in *Idaho County Voices,* p. 230, and Johnny Carrey and Cort Conley, *River of No Return,* p. 253, for more about the Irwins.

[2] All quotes from Opal and Gus Carlson are from the interview which took place at the Carlson home in Riggins, Idaho, September 3, 1985.

[3] Some of Gus Carlson's stories appeared in M. Bennett, "Windy Stories from the Salmon River," *Northwest Folklore,* Vol. 7 Fall 1988, No. 1, pp. 21–29.

[4] For comparable stories see Richard Bauman, "Any Man Who Keeps More'n One Hound'll Lie to You," in *And Other Neighborly Names,* ed. Richard Bauman and Roger D. Abrahams (Austin and London: University of Texas Press, 1981).

[5] "The Dog That Came Down Center" could be indexed under K 130, "Sale of worthless animals."

[6] See Carrey and Conley, *River of No Return,* 250. They give the location for Brundage's grazing area as Shorts Bar.

[7] "The Deef Fellows" can be indexed under XIII 3, "Two persons believe each other deaf." A trickster tells each of two persons before they meet that the other is hard of hearing and must be shouted at. A great shouting takes place and each thinks the other is out of his mind.

[8] Type 1698 C in Aarne and Thompson, *The Types of the Folktale,* is applicable to "The Deef Fellows."

[9] See Elsensohn, *Pioneer Days in Idaho Country,* 254–256, for an extensive description of Fred Burgdorf's resort, the hotel at Burgdorf. She relates that Burgdorf married an actress, Janette Foronsard of Denver, who was fond of lovely things including the unusual furniture made from lumber from the peculiarly knotted trees that grew on their place.

[10] For an interesting discussion of how the behavior of such local characters as the Jewetts functions in community stories to express values and norms, see Mullen, *I Heard the Old Fisherman Say,* 114–129.

Part Three

Ringer Family Narrators

Chapter Thirteen:
Elbra Harrah Brown

I've always been sad I didn't keep a diary. I could have prettinear wrote a book. I remember the first day I went to school. Was in the summer. Went down to the Large's, the neighbors of ours about two miles down the river. Didn't have no schoolhouse or place for school, so the four of us kids just sat under the pear trees. There wasn't many people around us, you know. We just had ourselves to play. We didn't know any different because we hadn't lived around other people.

—Elbra Harrah Brown, 1985

When I returned from my weekend along the Salmon, I was very encouraged by my findings, and found myself wishing I had been able to spend more time there with Salmon River tellers. Then I realized that near the school where I taught in North Bend, Washington, there were more potential tellers, Martha Ringer and her sisters. I jumped at an invitation to go and meet with Martha and three of her sisters, Elbra Harrah Brown, Gladys Harrah Mitchell, and Alice Harrah Hearing. These women were four of the twelve Harrah children who grew up in the hills above the Salmon River near Slate Creek. When I visited the Salmon country in 1995, Ron Mahurin had pointed out to me the site of their homestead. Previously, Martha had shared with me a picture of the old place taken in the 1890s. Wilbur and Katherine Harrah came with the oldest children from Oregon by covered wagon.

Site of Harrah homestead (upper right)
Photo MHB 1995

I was able to interview the four sisters at Martha's home in North Bend on October 12, 1985, a day when they had gotten together to make fudge for the senior citizen center Christmas bazaar. At that time Martha said there were six girls and one boy still living. They had remained in close contact. Alice Harrah Hearing said, "I don't think you could have a closer family than our family."[1] According to Martha, their storytelling activity had been an important part of creating and maintaining that family bond.

Alice Harrah Hearing, Martha Harrah Ringer, Elbra Harrah Brown, Gladys Harrah Mitchell (seated)
Photo MHB October 12, 1985

During my visit with the four Harrah sisters, I learned that they viewed their lives along the Salmon as being like a story. Martha said, "Do you ever watch *Little House on the Prairie*? That's just what it was like." It was revealing to me that Martha thought of their lives as being framed like the stories in the television series. Mary Auvil repeated this idea when I interviewed her in January 1996. I asked her why she thought Del Ringer's stories were so charming. She replied:

> Well, I think part of it for me, although it doesn't explain why you liked hearing them over and over, was just it was something you could imagine yourself being in. I guess the same reasons people like to watch *Little House on the Prairie*. It's kind of a nostalgia, wanting to hear about the good old days and things like that.[2]

The entire Harrah family evidently was adept at framing personal experience stories and anecdotes. In this group of the four sisters' stories, while the topics were all told from a woman's point of view, it was clear that the sisters were participating in a tradition that produced male tellers in the family. Martha related that her one living brother, Ray Harrah, was a great storyteller when he was younger. At age ninety-seven, Elbra was the oldest of the Harrah sisters. She was the one who engaged in storytelling most often when we met on that October afternoon. Her memory of the journey from Oregon in the covered wagon with her two younger brothers, father, and mother was "just like last week," she reminisced. Here is Elbra's adventure as she told it in an extended, multi-episode, personal-experience story:

"The Trip from Oregon"
Elbra Harrah Brown, 1985

We left Oregon.
My mother had three sisters
    who lived in the neighborhood.
They were about to leave.
Oh,
I remember it just like it was last week!

So the sisters came,
    and all the little kids,
    and,
oh,
we was havin' such a good time.
    and all the little girls wore bonnets then,
    and the strings some way came off my bonnet.

So I run in
    to have mom sew the strings on my bonnet.
She was cryin',
    and thought to myself,
        "Why is Mom cryin'?"
Of course,
I didn't realize what it meant to her,
    because she didn't know when she'd see her folks again.

Then I remember
we went down as far as the river,
    and the wind was a-blowin'
    and I guess there was maple trees,
    and my little brother.

    (What was he?
    I guess four.
    No, maybe about three)
    and if he saw a feather,
        or a leaf blow up
    he was there to get it.)

I remember that,
    and I remember the river.
I remember seeing all that.

So we kids did that on the way
    until we got to White Bird.

Then the Salmon River was up so high
    we had to camp there.

My father had picked out our place,
    and planned on
    going in the sheep business.
It was a nice big farm,
    but then the cattlemen found out
    we was going in there with sheep,
they put a stop to that.

So there we was with a nice big farm
    and nothin' to go into,
    and little kids.
So we just had a few cattle, a few pigs,
    just a little farm.

But I remember the day we got there.
We got to where the water was so high,
    and up onto the hill.
    I guess you can still see
    "the old high water trail" they called it.

Dad had gone up several times,
    while we were camped down by White Bird,
but he had to use the "high water trail."
So Dad was afraid
    to take us kids through the water,
    and there was an old Indian squaw there.
So she said
    Shoot, she'd go ahead.
    She wasn't afraid.
 So she took me on her horse,
    on the back of it.

Then I can't remember any more
    until we got up there.
So we got there,
    and this was home!!

We lived in a tent all summer.
People didn't know any different then.
It was how a lot of people lived.

But our dad, went and sawed trees down.
  I don't know how far he went.
Made a sled and hauled 'em down.

He had a horse by fall,
    So we got along.
We thought that was fine.

I was only about five years old
    when we left Oregon.
Now when I think of it
it makes me mad at myself
    that I didn't get a diary.
Now when I think of it
    when we moved in that place,
of course I was only five,
I just thought,
but I wasn't excited,
    "Well, this is where
    we are goin' to live."

What puzzles me is some parts is so clear,
Just like goin' down a road—
    nothin' to see,
    and then lots to see.
(I just remember the Indian lady so well.
    She wasn't afraid.
    "I'll take her across.")

What puzzles me,
    is now-a-days
    they have so many things to work with.

Dad had his little saw.
Just got up to the mountain,
    and haul 'em down
    and build a house.

Now they have all those machines.

What puzzles me now
  is how Mom did that.
Raised her family up there in the hills,
  and didn't complain.

Elbra Harrah Brown at ninety-seven years
Photo MHB 1985

Like the other narrators I recorded, Elbra's vocabulary consisted of common, ordinary, short words, and colloquial forms. She used the present for past like Alice Mahurin in such lines as, "so I run in to have Mom sew the strings on my bonnet," or, "just got up to the mountain, and haul 'em down and build a house." She had a distinctive personal style in framing her story. While there was little dialogue in this story, there were lines of interior speech filtered through her memory that moved it close to scene, for example:

I thought to myself, I wonder why mom is cryin'.
So she said, shoot, she'd go ahead. She wasn't afraid.
So we got there, and this was home.
I just thought, well, this is where we are going to live.
She wasn't afraid, I'll take her across.

These lines of interior monologue were effective in creating a unique dreamlike quality in the telling of this story. It was soft, filtered thought, more like the fuzzy edges of a dream than direct speech. I found her poetic in the repeated lines, "What puzzles me," "now when I think of it," and "I remember." Elbra used a poignant extended simile:

What puzzles me is some parts is so clear,
    and others there is a long space,
Just like going down a road—
    nothin' to see,
    and then lots to see.

Elbra presented herself as a major character and participant observer in the series of descriptions of scenes, e.g., taking her bonnet to her mother, her little brother's chasing the leaf, crossing the river, and her first impression of the home. Elba interwove commentary before and after each scene. It was a storytelling style that was unique to her, and very unlike the styles of her brother-in-law, Del Ringer, and the other tellers I had met.

While Elbra was the dominant solo storyteller in the session with the four sisters, some of the stories were told with the other sisters adding a line or two. When Elbra took the floor, however, the others yielded to her, suggesting that she traditionally held the role of primary storyteller of their common past. When I remarked about this fact, Elbra said to me that perhaps the reason for this was that, because she was the oldest and spent more time alone, things may have seemed clearer to her. She said, "For a while there was just my brother and I, and we was the only ones. Then when they came along, they could talk things over. Maybe they didn't notice everything like I did."

Elbra was very much a woman's storyteller if we consider the expression of emotions a feminine trait. She spoke of emotions, thoughts, and feelings, elements not present in other tellers thus far. Elbra liked to explain why her characters felt as they did. She realized that her mother was crying because she was leaving her family. She told of her father's fear of taking the children across the river himself. We learned of the family's disappointment and concern over their predicament when pressure from the cattlemen seemed to preclude their raising sheep as planned. We learned that these people accepted the hardships of life, and did not feel their lives were out of the ordinary.

Her stories were filled with the discussion of values. She admired her father's ability to create a home with only one small saw instead of all the equipment we have today. She marveled at her mother's ability to raise a family in the Idaho hills without complaint. Martha was right when she said, "it was just like *Little House on the Prairie*." These are precisely the sort of values presented in the television series. Certainly, one of Elbra's unique features was this penchant for devoting a large part of her story to articulating these beliefs. The fact that a story was told in order to present such values is not a unique feature to her. Del Ringer and the other narrators used their stories to present views on life; yet none made their commentaries as detailed and extensive as did Elbra. In the case of the men, the actions of the story expressed the worldview rather than direct statement.

The next personal experience story Elbra told was about a time when the family was afraid. It was interesting to note that, as a marker to denote the beginning of a story, Elbra used the line, "One exciting time I remember as if it was last week." This type of memory opening I realized was one of her personal style markers.

"The Indian Scare"
Elbra Harrah Brown, 1985

One exciting time
    I remember as if it was last week.
We was just little kids.

We saw these Indians on the big hill
    right in front of our place.
    And they was goin' up that hill so slow,
    and watchin' down there.

Then they'd get off their horses.
They wore blankets around them.

Mom was afraid they was watchin' us kids,
    and they was goin' to steal us.
So she kept 'em in.

Then here come them Indians,
    and they had made things.
They was to see the size of us.
They made moccasins and gloves for Dad.

I can just see them Indians look
    at the baby's little feet.

We was just out playing around,
    and they was just a-watchin' us
        to see how many we were,
    and how big we were!

They got to be real friendly.

I recalled that Mary Auvil had recorded from Del Ringer his memories about the Indians making gloves and moccasins for his family. Del related to Mary that there was one old squaw who had an old sewing machine that the head turned with a little crank. I wondered if she could have been one of the Indian squaws in Elbra's story. Del said:

When she made her gloves, she made you put your hand down and then she'd trace around your fingers. That was the bottom half. Then she'd lay the top half on and then stitch it, stitch with red silk thread. Jesus, they were pretty all beaded in solid white, then with that cockeyed deer head beaded on there.

This time there were no examples of interior monologue, although the line, "they was just a-watchin' us to see how many we were, and big we were," suggested interior thought. She continued to use her pattern of brief description of scene with some commentary about feelings. Her purpose of the story seemed to have been to show the Indians in a good light, and that her mother's and the children's fears were unnecessary although real.

The last story Elbra shared was about her feeling of longing for a precious orange she had received long ago on a rare visit to White Bird. An orange was a rare delicacy on the frontier. Again, we find her own typical beginning of "I remember":

"The Orange"
Elba Harrah Brown, 1985

I remember
it just as though it was last year.
I was seven,
    and so there was goin' to be a new baby

Dad was goin' to town,
    and Mom couldn't go.
So Dad took me down to White Bird
    so I could see what goes on around,
    and I was so bashful
    I couldn't talk to people.
Dad went
    and bought the biggest orange he could get,
    and gave me that.
I wouldn't open that orange
    for fear of gettin' something
    on my new dress mommy had made.
So I gave that orange away
            to another little girl
            and oh,
I have wanted that orange ever since!

This little reminiscence was primarily an incident Elbra told to describe her feelings. This brief story consisted of the description of the scene in which her father buys her the orange, followed by her commentary. It approaches the lyric end of the spectrum from narrative to lyric language.

An evaluation was implied that a little country girl who had never experienced much of a town should be pitied in her awkwardness and fears. The story had the pathetic humor of the adult looking back at the foolishness of the child in one's self. It shared with Del Ringer's stories a description of the awkward behavior of country folk in town. One thinks of the Berlinghoff brothers and their lack of know-how in town, or of Bill Jewett's visit to the hardware store to get "that new-fangled roofing." Thus, Elbra's story seemed derived from the same demographic pattern. It was a fact of life that many of these isolated people came to town rarely, and were somewhat overwhelmed by the experience. Their naiveté made a subject for a good story, even if it was a story about oneself.

I found Elbra to be a unique narrator showing her personal creativity within the larger traditions of the valley. In common with other local narrators, she shared the techniques of sparse use of detail in a series of scene descriptions, and repetition of key phrases and sentence patterns. She differed from the others in her use of interior monologue, and the emphasis on feelings and commentary, which gave her stories a lyric quality. Unlike the other women narrators, Alice Mahurin and Gay Robie, whose insistence on truth led them to eschew value statements, Elbra Brown's stories included evaluative comments. What she shared with all the other narrators was the fact that the stories were told to illustrate personal values. While her personal style differed, this common goal was apparent. She was a remarkable and distinctive storyteller.

On April 17, 1988, I had the privilege of attending Elbra's one hundredth birthday party, shortly before she passed on.

Elbra's one hundredth birthday party:
Elbra Brown, Alice Hearing, Gladys Mitchell,
Martha Ringer (standing), Maude Ekland (standing)
Photo courtesy Martha Ringer

Chapter Thirteen Notes

[1] The quotes from the Harrah sisters in this chapter are from the October 12, 1995 recording session at Martha Ringer's home in North Bend, Washington.

[2] The interview with Mary and Ken Auvil took place at their home in Soquel, California, January 1, 1986.

Chapter Fourteen:
Gladys Harrah Mitchell
and Alice Harrah Hearing

Our brother over in, Idaho, boy, he can just sit down
and tell you things. He remembered things. Boy, he
used to love to tell you things.—Alice Harrah Hearing,
1985

I can't remember a whole lot, but I remember ridin' the
horses. And I remember we slept in the loft, two, three
and as many as we could get in one bed. I remember
one time goin' to see one of my girl friends. Why there
was six in the bed. We slept crossways, and we thought
we had fun.

—Gladys Harrah Mitchell, 1985

Since Elbra was the major participant in the October 1985 interview
session, there was only limited involvement by the other sisters. While
I only got minuscule story samples from Gladys Harrah Mitchell and
Alice Harrah Hearing, they indicated that such family stories as theirs
were a part of the repertoires of all the Harrah sisters and their brothers
as well. I, therefore, felt Alice and Gladys's stories were significant in
my search for Salmon River storytelling traditions.

Gladys, ninety years old at the time of our recording, was recovering from the effects of a stroke that left her with some speech disability. She did not participate as fully in our session as she might have done before her stroke. I asked her if she knew the Jewetts and she replied, "They were just different from everybody else. Anything they did was different from what ordinary people did."[1] Gladys was alert, and interested in our discussion, and contributed two brief stories. The first was a humorous little incident about Martha's childhood.

"Martha's Kittens"
Gladys Harrah Mitchell, 1985

I can still see Martha comin' down the hill,
    and she had her dress up,
    and I thought,
    "Now what's she got?"

And what do you suppose
    she had found?
Some little baby skunks!
She thought
she had found some little kittens.

Our older brother told her to take
    all those pretty little kittens to the girls.
And he drowned all of 'em
    to get rid of 'em,
and oh, how she cried.

It was sad.

She thought
she had found some little kittens.

Gladys Harrah Mitchell, 1985
Photo MHB

Similar to Elbra's style, Gladys's story consisted of a scene and commentary. There was a line of interior monologue in, "Now what's she got?" She used a rhetorical question, "And what do you suppose she had found?" There was repetition of the line, "She thought she had found some little kittens." It was the relating of a dreamlike memory that could easily be mistaken for one of Elbra's stories. The opening line was similar to the type Elbra used to open her stories. The next story Gladys told was one I had previously heard told by Alice Mahurin.

"Lightning Kills Virgil"
Gladys Harrah Mitchell, [2] 1985

He was standin' on top of the haystack
 with a pitchfork in his hand.
We was havin' a waterspout
 with lightning.

The last words
   our oldest brother said he said
seems like they was just knocked out of his throat.
It came right down his fork,
   but it never set the hay on fire.

He was just a young boy.
That was Virgil.
Marvin was the oldest.

It was a big loss.

Hayfields along the Salmon
Photo MHB 1995

Virgil Harrah's grave
Photo MHB 1985

In these two brief samples from Gladys, I noted the same tendency toward a simple concrete vocabulary that characterized all the other narrators from this region. Like the previous story, this one consisted of a scene and commentary. Gladys included an evaluative comment, "It was a big loss." There was a simile-like feature, as Gladys described how the words seemed "knocked from his mouth." Like Elbra's, Gladys's stories emphasized feelings. I found this story moving in its simplicity.

It was not clear whether Gladys was present at this event; probably not, as the story must have first been told by Marvin because the remarks were attributed to him. Since I personally know of the story's being performed at least four times (by Marvin, by Alice Mahurin, by Gladys, and by Martha), I feel confident that it must have been a well-known story in the valley tradition.

Gladys's sister, Alice Harrah Hearing, eighty-eight at the time of the recording, told only one story. In great contrast to the last community-based story, this story was not well known in the valley, but only to family members.

"Martha's Baby"
Alice Harrah Hearing,[3] 1985

Our youngest sister died
    when she was seventeen in childbirth.
She died from a hemorrhage.

She seemed to know,
    and she and Martha were very close.

She told Martha,
    "Will you take my baby?"

    and then it just seemed
        she flew away.

Martha had lost her baby,
    and she took Norma.

It just seemed it was planned that way.

Martha Ringer and Alice Hearing
Photo MHB 1985

I found this little reminiscence by Alice dramatic and moving. It was a plainly told story. Only the word "hemorrhage" was longer than most words found in the speech of the valley narrators. As far as literary framing, it was not clear whether Alice was a participant observer in this event, or was relating a family story. The story just consisted of scene description and commentary. The one line of dialogue was the climax of the story. Her line, "and then it just seemed she flew away," implied the analogy of an angel or bird.

This was a very private story. Neither Del nor Martha, nor any of the family, ever mentioned that the Ringers had adopted Norma in our many conversations through the years. Martha revealed Norma's adoption to me in 1995. At that time Martha gave me the picture of all her sisters and pointed out Norma's birth mother, Georgie, the youngest sister in the far right of the front row. While Del chose mainly to tell of humorous or action filled events, it appeared the women in the family preferred stories that displayed their personal feelings and quite serious subjects.

Alice died in 1991. Gladys passed away at the age of ninety-seven on November 24, 1993. Here is photo of the Harrah girls given to me by Martha Ringer.

The eight Harrah sisters:
Gladys, Violet, Martha, Gertrude (top);
Alice, Elbra, Maude, Georgia (bottom)
Photo courtesy Martha Ringer

Chapter Fourteen Notes

[1] See Mullen, *I Heard an Old Fisherman Say*, 116–7, for a discussion on how local character anecdotes are based on behavior of individuals who are seen by the community as deviating from "ordinary folks" and are, as Gladys says, "different from everybody else."

[2] Gladys Harrah Mitchell was born December 1, 1895. She passed away at age ninety-seven on November 24, 1993, in Spokane, Washington.

[3] Alice Harrah Hearing, born May 13, 1897, died in North Bend, Washington, on March 18, 1991. She was ninety-three years old. Alice was the primary care giver for the younger Harrah children after her mother died in 1918 and the family moved to Spokane. Alice continued her care of others throughout her life: her nephews from the Spokane area, her husband Grover due to infirmity for several years before his death, and her older sister Elbra for a time. Georgie died November 26, 1926.

Chapter Fifteen:
Martha Harrah Ringer

We never saw a doctor when we was kids. Mother took
care of us. She'd make horehound and sage tea. You
can imagine why our mother passed away so young.
She was forty-eight. Had twelve children, babies just
born at home with midwife, Mrs. Large, hand sewing,
washing on the board.

—Martha Ringer, October 1985

Martha confirmed my suspicion that the story of her sister's death in
childbirth has always been a very private story when I visited her in her
trailer home in North Bend Washington, on September 17, 1995. She
made this remark about Georgie's death: "A lot of people don't realize
this or know it, and I never talk about it, but she [as she pointed to
her daughter Norma who had just stopped by] knows about it." Her
daughter, Norma Day, who had a trailer nearby, was present. Martha,
commenting that day about their strong family bonds, said, "We was
such a close family 'cause we lived up there in the hills and didn't
see a lot of people. We all helped one another." Martha and Norma
generously shared family photos from the past for this book. As she
pointed out Georgie in a family picture, Martha told the poignant
story of Georgie's death which occurred November 26, 1926. Sixty-
nine years later, it still brought tears to Martha's eyes.

"Georgie's Death"
Martha Ringer, 1995

She died in childbirth,
you know.

There were so many little kids,
we each took care of one.

One time, she turned to me.
She was usually with Maude,
but Maude slapped her hand,
    or did something one day.
And she hung on to me
    from that time on.

We went to this picnic
and I was settin' there holding her.

Dad came over,
"Here let me have her,
You go play with the other kids."
I went over there,
but I looked over there
and there she was a-cryin' and reachin' for me.

I couldn't stand it.
I went back over there and got her,
and sat there a-holdin' her.
I didn't want to leave her.

Well, when it was right at the last,
before her baby.
I was living in Yakima.
Gladys called me,
"Martha, Georgie is real bad.
She wants to see you."

I went to Spokane.
Got over there in the morning,
she said,

"I'm goin' to die,
     If I die, will you take care of my baby?"

So we adopted her.
When her husband came in,
after the doctor pronounced her,
he said,
"I couldn't go against the words
of dead person's wishes."
So we just adopted her right then,
made her ours.
Georgie was just seventeen
when her baby was born.

(My mother died young, too.)

She was just a kid,
died so young,

Too young.

Georgia Harrah as a young girl
Photo courtesy Martha Ringer and Norma Day

Martha told me other stories of family deaths that day. Georgie was only eight when their mother died. Her brother Lloyd was killed cleaning his gun on December 25, 1929. He was thirty-two years old. She said, "It was right close around Christmas. He lived over in Idaho there near Boise. They said he was cleaning his gun, you know. The gun went off and killed him. It was very sad."

Lloyd Harrah
Photo courtesy Martha Ringer

Here is her version of her brother Virgil's death on August 3, 1911, related to me earlier by Gladys at the time of the sisters' interview in 1985:

"Virgil's Death"
Martha Ringer, 1995

Virgil was killed by lightning.
He was probably eighteen or so.

It was raining you know.
They was starting to work the hay.

My dad hadn't proved up
    on the place.
Elba was old enough, so
they took it.

The boys was up there working.
The boys, Marvin and Virgil,
    were out working.

It started to rain,
    then it would quit,
you know how it is.

He called out to Marvin,
    "Well, I think it's quit rainin',
    we can start workin'…"
Marvin said,
    He was just cut off.
    He couldn't hear what he said.

There was a streak of lightning,
the lightning killed him.

He was gone that quick.

Stories about unusual death seemed to be part of the repertoire of many of the tellers. Gus Carlson, Delbert Wicks, and the Robies mentioned the death of Old Man Jewett by the rattlesnake, and it was one of Del's frequently told stories. Gay Robie told of John Kimbrough's death. Martha Ringer, Gladys Brown, and Alice Mahurin all told of Virgil Harrah's death. Ron Mahurin had a number of stories about the various gravesites in the valley. Martha told about Old Lady Jewett's disappearance and apparent demise as follows:

"Mrs. Jewett Disappeared"
Martha Ringer, 1995

The Jewetts was an odd sort of family.
Mrs. Jewett just disappeared.
They never knew what became of her.
They never could find her body or nothin'.

She went for a ride one day, and
    never showed up again.
They never knew what happened to her,
whether she got lost back in the hills
    and died or what.

She just disappeared.

Earlier Alice Mahurin had told me of her father, Ed Robie's, tragic accident. Martha also recounted to me the story of Ed Robie's death which occurred in 1920. Here is Martha's version:

"The Death of Ed Robie"
Martha Harrah Ringer, October 1985

Ed Robie was a big, tall skinny guy.
They lived up there in the hills
    back of Slate Creek.
I don't know what he was doin',
but he went off lookin' for stock or something,
and he called to his wife,
and said,
"Put on the coffee pot.
I'll be back in a little bit."
He went out to get on the horse,
and it had been a horse he was breaking,
and he used to even take the baby
    on this horse with him
and they'd go for a ride,
but he called to her,
    "Put on the coffee pot.
I'll be back in a little bit."

She thought he sounded kind of funny,
and she looked out,
and his foot was caught in the stirrup,
and the horse went up and down the hill,
and just *drug him to death.*

Not all her stories were so serious. Martha told a story on the lighter side. The following personal experience showed her ability to make a humorous story of a frightening experience:

"The Big Storm"[1]
Martha Ringer, October 1985

I remember when
Del and I was married a couple of years,
we lived up on the hill above Slate Creek with his dad.
We lived up there,
and his mother and dad
        was back in the mountains looking after cattle.

There come this awful storm,
thunder and lightning,
and about that time the neighbor come up,
and said,
Del's grandmother was sick,
and they wanted him to come.

My little niece was there with us,
        and he was gone overnight.

It was so bad in the house we was living in.
Here was this main part of the house,
and then was the part with the kitchen and dining room.
and I told my niece,
        "Well, we'll go out there
        where it isn't so bad."
Well, I went into the bedroom to get my clothes,
and it looked like someone had taken a knife around the ceiling.
The whole thing was lying on the floor!

I couldn't sleep a wink that night.
All I could think about
    was Del going up there on the ridge.
They made it home alright.
They laughed at me.
They had a milk cow,
and somehow she was over the fence,
and I told Del,
    "I don't know how she got over there.
The wind blew her."
They always laughed
about the wind a-blowin' the cow.

While her husband was alive, Martha rarely volunteered any stories in our recording sessions, though it was obvious that she knew all the stories and would frequently prompt Del. He was clearly the one with the reputation for storytelling, and therefore had the spotlight. It was not until the interview with her sisters after his death that Martha revealed herself as a storyteller. In the session with her sisters, Martha contributed significantly and convinced me that under certain circumstances, she could be a moving storyteller. In 1996 at age ninety-four, her ability to tell an engaging story about the old days along the Salmon had not dimmed.

Chapter Fifteen Notes

[1] "The Big Storm" is related to xx1611.1, "Lies about big wind (cyclone, tornado)."

Chapter Sixteen:
Salmon River Storytelling Style

"The Guts Is on the Bottom"
Dig, deep. The guts is on the bottom.
—Del Ringer, 1965

Well, one thing I will say. My mind hasn't gotten that bad.
—Del Ringer, 1985

(Commenting at our last interview on his
ability to tell stories at age eighty-five.)

I had come to end of my quest to answer the question: Was there a community storytelling style influencing Del Ringer's crafting of his tales? The answer was yes. I was satisfied that through my examination of the stories gathered from his family and the Idaho narrators, I had established that Del Ringer's storytelling style definitely shared aspects of a "Salmon River" community style.[1] One could continue this quest more extensively along the river. I hope to return someday soon and probe further into more windy stories from the Salmon River country.

Here are the conclusions about individual and community storytelling styles that I believe are revealed in these stories: At the surface level of vocabulary and speech patterns, Del and all of the narrators shared the fact that their rather limited story vocabularies consisted of concrete, short, common words, used frequently with some substandard grammar. There were favorite local word forms and fillers. They were important in the flavor they added to the stories.

At the level of the literary styling, while there was evidence of common traits, narrator choices were more idiosyncratic. Most tellers shared with Del the characteristic use of sparse descriptive detail. Del and most of the narrators shunned more than the occasional use of literary devices such as metaphor, simile, and cliché. Repetition and irony were common to the stories of most of the narrators.

I found much individuality in the choices the narrators made about framing a story. Some chose to tell it in scenes through dialogue; others simply told a story by recounting the action. Presenting the high points of the story in scenes through dialogue was characteristic of Del and Martha Ringer, Gus Carlson, Delbert Wicks, and John Day. Gay Robie, the Mahurins, and the Harrah sisters preferred to tell stories using some indirect discourse, or even interior monologue along with description. The Harrah sisters all used a pattern of scene description and comments on feelings, with great emphasis on emotional content. Gay Robie and Alice Mahurin shared the insistence on truth, and telling stories through description of the action rather than by using dialogue.

Here are a few examples of individual creativity within the broader tradition: Both Martha Ringer and Alice Mahurin told versions of the "Death of Ed Robie." Alice simply related the action of what happened. Martha's story was more compelling for me because of the dialogue quotes she chose to repeat. These were Ed's last words to his wife: "Put on the coffee pot. I'll be back in a little bit." Mrs. Benedict's story as told by Alice Mahurin and the one told by Del Ringer were very different. While Alice's version probably came closest to the truth of what really happened, Del's choice of dialogue and detail made his version more suspenseful and interesting. I found the Harrah sisters' technique of story and commentary on the emotions very appealing; yet, I also enjoyed totally different styles in Del's action-packed adventures, and Gus Carlson's long, episodic journey tales. Thus, the individual artistic styling of the tellers was more visible at this level of literary framing than it was at the surface level of vocabulary choices and speech patterns, which showed far reaching cultural trends. I might add, however, that an artist like Del Ringer could take even those common speech patterns and words and give them surprising fresh twists, as in the statement, "she cussed him black and blue."

The features of actual oral presentation varied with the personalities of the tellers, and individual artistry contributed to the impact of the stories on the listeners. Regional patterns seemed unimportant. Gus Carlson, Ron Mahurin, and Gay Robie were all vigorous tellers who used gestures, considerable volume, rapid delivery rate, and much vocal variation. Del Ringer and the Harrah sisters exhibited a much quieter, subdued style. Alice Mahurin presented her stories in a monotone. Delbert Wicks droned as well. Each presentational style seemed suited to the teller. Some simply used more gestures and physical, facial, and vocal expression than others. It was strictly a matter of individual preference and artistry in these oral performance styles, and not really indicative of valley performance style.

The really major commonalities of community style emerged at the folkloric level in the characters, themes, and attitudes presented in the stories. At this level, and not surprisingly, because of the very nature of folklore to sustain tradition, the strong power of the local story patterns over the tellers could be felt. It still amazes me that I found people storying fifty years later about the same characters that Del Ringer had used. Here was Ron Mahurin, a comparatively young man, telling stories about playing tricks on the Jewetts similar to Del's tricks on them. It was significant that both Del Ringer and Alice Mahurin told the story of Mrs. Benedict. Del's story of Old Man Jewett's death as the result of a rattlesnake bite was told by a number of the narrators. The Jewetts were also found in the stories of Delbert Wicks and Gus Carlson. The death of Ed Robie was the subject of stories by Martha Ringer and Alice Mahurin. John Phelan, the sheepherder, and John Kimbrough, the walking bank, appeared in stories by Gay Robie and Gus Carlson. The trend toward common subjects and characters that have sustained a long period in oral tradition was indisputably in evidence.

At the level of story themes and attitudes, Del Ringer shared undeniably with others of this community. There was the theme of respect for courage in the face of danger from wild animals or irate neighbors. There was admiration for the honesty of those who worked hard and persevered in spite of ridicule, as did Henry Ricke with his walnut trees, or Gus Carlson's thrifty uncle, John Kimbrough, or Gay Robie's honest dad as he sealed up the deceased Kimbrough's money briefcase. There was respect for people who lived by their values, as did the sheepherder John Phelan, or Old Man Wyatt, or even Del himself in John Day's stories. There was the persistent attitude concerning the necessity of proper behavior with ladies, as in Del's story about the Berlinghoff's courting, and in Del's and Gus Carlson's stories about the expulsion of the rowdies at the dances. Finally, there was amusement at greenhorn types, such as "The Dude," or the young Gus Carlson in "The Madame at Burgdorf," or even Del himself in "Dig Deep." I was able to locate many of these story patterns in the motif and story indexes indicating that they have wide distribution in folklore.[2] While these patterns enjoy much further distribution than the Salmon River Valley area, one can conclude that they were unquestionably in evidence in the tradition of the small area that served as the setting for most of the stories in this collection. Del Ringer clearly shared the significant commonalities of themes and attitudes with all the tellers I interviewed. These examples convinced me that these local story traditions wielded a powerful influence on the individual tellers.

It was also apparent that the Salmon River country has long nurtured a storytelling tradition. Many of the narrators spoke of the fact that during much of their lives, time was passed telling stories. It was an important behavior for them. Elbra wished that she had kept a diary to record them. Gus remembered the windy stories of Old Motts, and others that he wished he had written down. Gay said she recalled spending her time as a child listening to the sheepherders and other folks tell "cougar stories." Martha spoke fondly of the family potlucks and story sessions at Buena. Her grandchildren and nieces related how they loved the storytelling session of the elders. It was gratifying for me to verify this tradition of storytelling of personal narratives, and to ascertain that Del Ringer was only one of the many raconteurs produced by this Salmon River country.

For me Del will always remain the master storyteller of them all. He shines as surely one of the most gifted storytellers I have ever had the good fortune to meet. Only Gus Carlson proved to be his equal in creating entertaining dialogue and arresting stories. Del was extremely adept in his use of sparse detail in a cartoon-like manner to create an image, as in his description of Bill Jewett's eating when a little girl says, "Mama, Mama, them whiskers open up and the food goes in." He was a master in the use of irony to achieve humor, and excelled at telling stories involving some sort of ironic collusion in which someone was excluded from privileged knowledge the rest shared. Finally, I loved his fresh ways with simple words as in the expression, "He had a little one-room cabin not big enough to cuss a cat in."

One interesting and surprising finding about Del Ringer's storying concerns the effects of contexts on his telling. Mary Auvil recorded Del's stories on a family fishing trip in 1965 with a hidden microphone "under the bed." This was a natural context for him. My five interviews of Del Ringer were not in this normal family setting for his storying. Sometimes I brought someone "new" with me to provide Del with a new audience over time. Sometimes I was alone. Amazingly, his stories remained remarkably stable and consistent through all these tellings, and even with those recorded in his normal family setting by Mary Auvil. He added second episodes as the spirit moved him, but there was no pattern of progressively adding to or changing the stories over time. This was a surprising result considering the popular conception that stories grow and are embellished with repeated tellings. The fact that his stories remained so stable was a puzzling discovery, for it supports neither the belief in story embellishment over time nor the "devolutionary theory"[3] of folklore that suggests that forms of folklore deteriorate over time.

Another interesting finding about Del's storying, discovered through my analyses of his repeated versions of a single story, was that within Del's repertoire with each story had a story style. This confirms John Ball's hypothesis that in addition to individual and community style, one should be able to determine "the style of the story."[3] For example, in "The Hayracks" and "Jewett's Roof," Del supplied much more descriptive detail than most of his stories because physical construction was involved, and details had to be given for an understanding of how the Berlinghoffs and Jewetts "goofed" the projects. In most of his stories Del Ringer used irony, humor, and exaggeration. None of these were used in "The Indian War" because they did not fit the serious style of the story.

I was satisfied with my affirmative answer to the question: Did Del Ringer exhibit a community Salmon River as well as individual style in his storytelling? I found myself, however, speculating about another question: Why was this storying about life experiences so valued by Del Ringer and the other narrators that it was such an important persistent behavior for them? After much thought, I have come to some conclusions about the basic functions that such storying serves for us all. First of all, personal stories present our identities and values. Del Ringer's stories were a presentation of himself. As we listen to another's personal stories, we make an assessment of the values with which that person identifies. The stories are rarely neutral. They usually include some sort of evaluation about the point of the story. Listeners judge that evaluation and thereby the teller. Del Ringer's personality permeated all his stories. In coming to appreciate his stories, one came to appreciate him as a person and the values he stood for. He imbued his texts with his worldview and personality. It is not difficult to imagine his telling them with a twinkle in his eye, and to feel one knew him and what he stood for through his stories. Del seemed to me a person who came to old age in a state of what Erik Eriksen calls "ego integrity,"[5] as Del used his narratives to articulate and defend his values. It just might be that the ability to reminisce and frame one's life experience into meaningful narratives is conducive to good mental health. I believe Del Ringer and the other narrators used storying about life to give order and meaning to their life experiences. It appears this behavior functioned well for them in achieving a sense of unity and well-being.

Secondly, I believe Del and the others told their stories as a way of helping to preserve the values of the community. Part of the general nature of folklore lies in its support of the status quo attitudes of a community. Del Ringer's stories not only presented his personal values but, as was also shown in the narratives from the community raconteurs, his values were representative of those commonly held in the community. Both his niece and grandson commented that his stories were little parables about proper behavior. It is clear that Del Ringer shared his attitudes about behavior with the other storytellers, and that they all felt it was important to articulate these shared values.

A third function that such stories serve appears to be that of encouraging bonding between persons. It seems evident that the telling of personal stories can be very influential in creating family and community ties. All members of Del Ringer's family that I met indicated that sharing through storytelling helped create their strong family bond. In making oneself vulnerable through telling personal stories, trust is created, which produces feelings of closeness. I believe that particularly influential in creating these feelings of closeness are shared stories from one's youth. It appears individuals are more open to bonding at that period than in later life. In my own life I feel a deep kinship with the people I grew up with in my hometown of two thousand people, yet I do not know many of the dozen or so families who live on my lane today. The bonds seem very strong indeed with people with whom we share a past. This finding could explain why Del Ringer chose life along the Salmon in his youth, rather than his adult life in logging in Washington, as the subject for his stories. When I asked Mary and Ken Auvil in our 1986 interview why Del never told stories about North Bend, Mary replied:

> I remember vaguely him telling about a couple of people there, but they weren't the kind he repeated over and over again. I think when you are young people make a stronger impression on you. It might have been an age thing, or maybe just the charm of that place. I think maybe it is because as a young person you just don't have as much access to other people.

Certainly the Ringer family glue appeared remarkably strong. I recalled again how Mary Auvil fondly reminisced about Del's telling stories to her dad and another uncle back in the 1940s when she was a child. Mary remembered, "We kids would hear them and say, now they are on old Buena, or Old Tom, or Old Bill Jewett, then it will be politics." Those memories were clearly very dear to her. In the October 1986 interview with Martha Ringer and her three sisters (still together as they approached the century mark), Martha said, "There couldn't be closer families than the Harrahs or the Ringers." It was obvious that keeping alive these stories about their experiences in their youth was important in the family bonding.

A fourth function that I feel personal stories serve is to offer a way to express and dissipate emotions by creating stories about those feelings and communicating them to others. In the stories told in the Harrah family about the deaths of the brothers, Virgil and Hal, and of their sister, Georgie, or Alice Mahurin's story about her father being dragged to death by his horse, grief has been transmuted into family stories. The emotion might be fear as in Del Ringer's stories "Kanky and the Mules" and "The Cougar Scare," or Martha Ringer's "The Big Storm," or Gay Robie's story "The Bear." The emotion might be longing as in Elba Brown's "The Orange."

It was noteworthy that the women storytellers commented on emotions directly, while Del and the other men dealt with emotions through the action of the stories. Also, the stories of the women narrators dealt with more serious subjects than the men's, and the Harrah sisters' stories revealed very private feelings. The men appeared to strive to be more objective; hence their use of the action filled story form.

Finally, the function of providing amusement though these narratives is not to be minimized. When I asked Ken Auvil why Del's stories were passed on he said, "I think it might have been because where you lived as a youngster certain stories made their rounds, and these stories were a prime event because you didn't have other kinds of entertainment." It appears that passing the time by telling personal stories is still a major activity in the Salmon River area, and with the members of Del Ringer's family even today. Del's grandson, John Day, still gets tremendous enjoyment from telling his own stories about what a character his Gramps was. Ron Mahurin enjoys "holding forth" at home with friends, or on an occasional visit to the local tavern. All of us, even those in the most sophisticated circles, seem to have our favorite windy stories of the days when we were young. These stories are shared just for the sheer enjoyment of the telling, and for the pleasure that they bring to others. Del Ringer was much sought out by members of his family and close community for the amusement value of his stories. Probably anyone would have relished the chance to sit down with him on the old stump in the pasture, as he did with his grandchildren, and pass the time of day listening to his stories of the good old days. One could have whiled away a pleasant afternoon with any of the narrators in this collection as they shared their stories of life along the Salmon.

My encounter with these Salmon River storytellers has been one of the peak experiences of my life. I'm glad I dug deep enough to "find the guts on the bottom" in the stories of these narrators. The "guts" are the fascinating bits of Americana revealed in these tales of life at the turn of the century along the Salmon River. When I stood in the old cemeteries above the Salmon River and saw the graves of many of the people in these stories, I was reminded of the voices from the dead which are presented in Edgar Lee Masters' *Spoon River Anthology* and Thornton Wilder's *Our Town*. I reflected, where are most of these people whose stories I had heard?

Many are sleeping on the hills along the Salmon. Edgar Lee Masters says in his poem "The Hill":

Where are Elmer, Herman, Bert, Tom and Charley?
   The weak of will, the strong of arm,
       the clown, the boozer, the fighter?
   All, all are sleeping on the hill.[6]

The stage manager in *Our Town* tells us:
   Over there are the old stones ... strong minded people that come
   a long way to be independent....

An awful lot of sorrow has sort of quieted up here....
We're all glad they are in a beautiful place,
   and we're coming up here ourselves when our fit is over.

They are waitin' for something that they feel is comin'.
   Something important and great.
Aren't they waitin' for the eternal part in them to come our clear?[7]

White Bird cemetery
Photo MHB 1995

Slate Creek cemetery
Photo MHB 1995

The voices of the people in the Salmon River stories, and those of many of my narrators, have now been stilled. It has been a privilege for me to have shared in the stories of these pioneers, and to learn of the joys and laughter, as well as the sorrows, of their lives. Hopefully the readers have been enriched as well by this opportunity to know through their windy stories Del Ringer and the Salmon River country storytellers.

Del would have said, "They were good old wagons, even if their wheels did rattle."

Good old wagons
Photo MHB 1995

Chapter Sixteen Notes

[1] For a more detailed account of the methodology used in this style search, see Marjorie Bangs Bennett, "Individuality and Community Style in Personal Narratives of Storyteller Del Ringer of North Bend, Washington" (PhD dissertation, University of Washington, 1986).

[2] See Stith Thompson, *Motif-Index*, and Aarne and Thompson, *The Types of the Folktale* (Folklore Fellows Communication No. 184), as well as, Baughman, *A Type and Motif-Index of the Folktales of England and North America.*

[3] See Alan Dundes, "The Devolutionary Premise in Folklore Theory," *Journal of Folklore Institute,* 3 (1966), pp. 226–49.

[4] Ball, "Style in the Folktale," 172.

[5] See Erik Erikson, *Childhood and Society* (New York: W.W. Norton, Inc., 1963), pp. 268–9.

[6] Edgar Lee Masters, *Spoon River Anthology* (New York: The Macmillan Company, 1958), p. 1.

[7] Thornton Wilder, *Our Town*, Richard Corbin and Miriam Balf, Editors, *12 American Plays* (New York: Charles Scribner's Sons, 1969), pp. 163–4.

Selected Bibliography
of Related Research

Aarne, Antti, and Thompson, Stith. *The Types of the Folktale.* Folklore Fellows Communication Vol. 184. Helsinki: Soumalainen Tiedeakagtemia, 1961.

Attebury, Jennifer. "Storytelling Style in the Personal Narratives of Homer Springs." *Journal of Folklore Institute,* Vol. XIV, 1977, pp. 31–49.

Attebury, Louie W., Editor. *Idaho Folklife: Homesteads to Headstones.* Boise, Idaho: University of Idaho, Salt Lake City, Utah: University of Utah Press, 1985.

Attebury, Louie W. *Sheep May Safely Graze: A Personal Essay on Tradition and a Contemporary Sheep Ranch.* Moscow, Idaho: University of Idaho Press, 1992.

Bailey, Robert G. *River of No Return (The Great Salmon River of Idaho).* Lewiston, Idaho: The R.G. Bailey Printing Company, 1947.

Ball, John, "Style in the Folktale," *Folklore,* Vol. 65, 1954.

Baughman, Ernest. *A Type and Motif Index of the Folktales of England and North America.* The Hague: Indiana University Folklore Series, 1966.

Booth, Wayne. *The Rhetoric of Fiction.* Chicago and London: University of Chicago Press, 1961.

Brunvand, Jan Harold. *The Study of American Folklore.* New York: W.W. Norton & Company, 1968.

Carrey, Johnny, and Cort Conley. *River of No Return .* Cambridge, Idaho: Backeddy Books, 1978.

Carrey, Johnny, Cort Conley, and Ace Barton. *The Snake River of Hells Canyon.* Cambridge, Idaho: Backeddy Press, 1979.

Chesdsey, Zona and Carolyn Frei, Editors. *Idaho County Voices.* Grangeville, Idaho: Idaho County Centennial Committee, 1990.

Deemer, Polly. "Style in the Anglo-American Legend." PhD dissertation. University of Oregon, 1975.

Dorson, Richard. "Oral Style of American Folk Narrators," *Folklore: Selected Essays,* Edited by Richard Dorson. Bloomington: Indiana University Press, 1972, pp. 99–146.

Edmundson, Munro S. *Lore: An Introduction to Language and Literature.* New York: Holt, Rinehart, & Wilson, 1971.

Elsensohn, Sister M. Alfreda. *Pioneer Days in Idaho Country,* Vol. One. Caldwell, Idaho: The Caxton Printers, Ltd., 1947.

Glassie, Henry. *Passing the Time in Ballymenone.* Philadelphia: University of Pennsylvania, Press, 1982.

Howard, Helen Addison, and Dan L. McGrath. *War Chief Joseph.* Caldwell, Idaho: The Caxton Printers, Ltd., 1958.

Kirkwood, Charlotte M. *The Nez Perce Indian War Under War Chiefs Joseph and White Bird,* Grangeville, Idaho: The Idaho Country Free Press, about 1948 (no date given). Printed by special permission of Mrs. Lenore Kirkwood Rogers, daughter of author.

Kirshenblatt-Gimblatt, Barbara. "Traditional Storytelling in the Toronto Jewish Culture." PhD dissertation. Bloomington, University of Indiana, 1972.

Labov, William, and Joshua Waletzky. "Oral Versions of Personal Experience." *Essays on the Verbal and Visual Arts.* Edited by June Helm. Seattle: University of Washington Press, 1967, pp. 12–44.

Manser, Eunice Clay, and Murrielle McGaffee Wilson. *Riggins on the Salmon River.* Weiser, Idaho: Signal-American Printers, 1983.

Mullen, Patrick B. *I Heard the Old Fisherman Say.* Austin and London: University of Texas Press, 1978.

Ong, Walter. "Oral Remembering and Narrative Structures." *Analyzing Discourse: Text and Talk*. Editor, Deborah Tannen. Georgetown: Georgetown University Roundtable on Language and Linguistitics, 1981.

Stahl, Sandra. "The Local Character Anecdote." *Genre*, Vol. 8, 1975, pp. 283–302

Stahl, Sandra. "The Oral Personal Narrative in its Generic Context". *Fabula*, Vol. 18, 1977, pp. 18–39.

Stahl, Sandra. "The Personal Narrative as a Folklore Genre." PhD dissertation. Indiana University, 1977.

Tedlock, Dennis. "On the Translation of Style in Oral Narrative." *Toward New Perspectives in Folklore*. Edited by Americo Paredes and Richard Bauman. Austin: University of Texas Press, 1972, pp. 121–30.

Thompson, Stith. *Motif Index of Folk Literature*. Revised and Enlarged Edition. Bloomington: Indiana University Press, 1955–58.

Toelken, Barre. *The Dynamics of Folklore*. Boston: Houghton Mifflin Co., 1975.

Wolfson, Ness. *CHP: The Conversational Historical Present in American English Narrative.* Topics in Sociolinguistics. Edited by Nessa Wolfson. Dordrecht-Holland/Cinnaminson-USA: Foris Publications, 1982.

List of Figures

Index

Photographs are indicated with a "*ph*" following the page number. Ex: 32*ph*.
Charts are indicated with a "*ch*" following the page number. Ex: 236ch
Notes are indicated by "page number+n+note number." Ex: 147n

buggy accident, 130–131
Bull Durham tobacco, 161
Burgdorf, Fred, 180n9
Burgdorf, Madame at, 166–171
Buying the Wind (Dorson), 90

C

cabin, old, 89*ph*
car, on White Bird Hill, 44*ph*
car battery, 44
Carlson, Gus, 3, 6, 161*ph*
    background of, 159–162
    on the C.C. camp, 159
    "Charlie Clay's Jail," 178–179
    death, stories about, 209
    death of, 179
    dialogue, recounting scenes through, 216
    "Dog That Came Down Center, The," 163
    "John Phelan Goes to Walla Walla," 173–176
    and John Kimbrough, 119
    "Madame at Burgdorf, The," 166–170
    and Alice Mahurin's style, 171
    and moonshiners, 177
    and Nez Perce Indians, 178
    oral presentation, 217
    personal experience narratives, 162
    and Del Ringer's style, 163, 165–166, 171, 177, 179
    and Gay Robie's style, 166, 171
    and sheepherding, 161–163
    stories, content of, 217–218
    style, episodic journey tales, 216
    "The Deef Fellows," 166, 180n7
    and Delbert Wick's style, 163
Carlson, Mick, 160
Carlson, Opal Patterson, 159–160, 162, 164–165, 177
Carrey, John, 122, 122*ph*, 171, 180n1
Carrey, Mary, 122*ph*
cartoon-like style, 97

Catholics, 80
cattle drive through White Bird (ID), 144*ph*, 154
cattlemen, 187, 190
Cayuse Mules, 48
cemeteries, local, 150
Chamberlain, William "Will," 16, 29n1
Chamberlain , Emily Robie, 129*ph*
character anecdote stories, 87–90
character voices, 171
"Charlie Clay's Jail" (Carlson), 178–179
Chicago (IL), 3
Chief Joseph, 69, 78, 81–84, 82*ph*, 84, 84*ph*, 147n8–148n8
Chief White Bird, 147n8–148n8
city-bred dudes, in stories, 45–48, 97–98, 112, 171, 179, 218
Clarke, Kenneth, ix–xi
Clarkston (WA), 15
Clay, Charlie, 178–179
clichés, 216
Colfax (WA), 15
colloquial forms, 138, 155, 189
Colville reservation (WA), 84
common speech patterns, 216–217
common words, use of, 109
community storytelling, 6, 9, 112, 215, 219–220, 226n1
concrete vocabulary, 96, 201
Conley, Cort, 32*ph*, 36*ph*, 122, 122*ph*, 180n1
Conne, Margaret Ellen. *see* Wyatt, Margaret Ellen Conne
"Cougar Scare, The" (Ringer, D.), 63–65, 222
cougar stories, 63–65, 106–107, 124–125, 218
country style humor, 96
cowboy stories, 123
cowboys, 32, 65–66, 162
cows, 64–65, 153–154, 156, 177, 212
coyotes, 63, 65, 66–67
Crane Creek (ID), 160
Crane Creek, homesteaders on, 104
cultural analysis, 7

D

"Dance with the Berlinghoffs" (Ringer, D.), 37–40, 52n3
dances
  community, 21
  and dance hall fights, 173, 178–179
  lady's choice, 53
  rowdies at, 218
  Saturday night, 36–38, 42
  at Women's Club, in Parker (ID), 92–96
Davis, Ben, 23
Davis, Clay, 34, 36*ph*, 42–44, 46–47, 134, 166
Davis, Emma, 36*ph*
Davis boys, in "The Pickled Peppers," 94–95
Day, Diana, 28
Day, John, 22, 26–27, 216, 218, 222
Day, Norma Ringer, 25–26, 202–203, 205, 207*ph*
death, stories about, 209
"Death of Ed Robie, The" (Ringer, M.), 210–211
"Deef Boy, The" (Robie), 124–125
"Deef Fellows, The" (Carlson), 166, 180n7
deer, 63, 65, 67–68, 70, 120
"Del Ropes a Coyote and a Deer" (Ringer, D.), 67–68
Depression, The, 104, 154–155, 162
descriptions, and emotional content, 216
descriptive details, 179
descriptive phrases, colorful, 8
devolutionary theory, 219
dialogue, 107, 109–111, 171, 189, 216
"Dog That Came Down Center, The" (Carlson), 163
dogs, 71, 105–106, 120–121, 153
Dorson, Richard, 90, 99
Downtown White Bird, 41*ph*
dramatizations, of dialogue lines, 109
"Dude, The" (Ringer, D.), 45–47, 52n4, 112

E

Edinburgh (Scotland), 116
Edmunson, Munro, 7, 11n3
"ego integrity," 220
Ekland, Maude, 194*ph*
elk stories, 63, 108, 115, 123
Elzroth, Nettie Rice, 14–16, 25, 78
Elzroth, Newt, 15–16, 25
emotions, 221–222
Eriksen, Erik, 220
E.S. Bergen Company, in Spokane (WA), 132
exaggeration, 219
experiences, peak, 222

F

family trees, 236*ch*–237*ch*
Ferris, Bill, 85
ferry across the Salmon River, 45*ph*
Fisherman's Hornpipe, The (song), 31
folk wisdom, 150
folklore, 4, 7, 97–98, 127, 218–220
Folklore, 9
Foronsard, Janette, 180
Foskett, Wilson, 21, 58–60, 60*ph*, 131, 142
framing the story, 8, 97, 139, 185
France, 116
Frank Wyatt's Ranch. *see* Wyatt, Frank
Frankie, Aunt, 136–138
French, Charlie, 176–177
French cemetery, 150
Frenchman, in "The Pickled Peppers," 92–93

G

"Georgie's Death" (Ringer, M.), 206–207
gloves, 70, 192
Gordon, Roy, 55
grammar, 216
Grand River (ID), 16
Grangeville (ID), 80, 131, 147n8–148n8

hayfields, along Salmon River, 200*ph*
haying, 23, 33–35, 35*ph,* 52n2, 199–
200, 209
"Hayracks, The" (Ringer, D.), 33–35,
219
Hearing, Alice Margaret Harrah, 29n2,
184*ph,* 202*ph,* 203*ph*
death of, 203, 204n3
and emotional content, 216
growing up, in Slate Creek (ID),
183
interior monologue, use of, 216
marriage of, 22–23
"Martha's Baby," 202
move to North Bend (WA), 26
oral presentation, 217
in school, with Del Ringer, 18
stories, repertoire of, 197, 201
storytelling style of, 203
Hearing, Grover, 22, 26, 204n3
herders. *see* sheepherders
hills above the Salmon River, 91*ph*
Hollenbeak, Loy, 103, 106–108, 113n2
barn, in Riggins (ID), 107*ph*
Hollenbeak barn, 107*ph,* 113n2
homesteaders
Gus Carlson's family as, 160
on Crane Creek, 104
Harrah family as, 20*ph,* 150, 183–
184, 184*ph*
Ron Mahurin's family as, 155*ph*
Henry Ricke family as, 87–88
Ringer family as, 5, 16, 91, 150
on Wyatt's ranch, 48–50
horses, 73, 75, 153, 170*ph*
horse-swapping, 71–76, 104, 162,
180n4
humor. *see also* jokes
American tradition of, 71
in Gus Carlson's stories, 175–176
in a frightening experience, 211
irony, use of, 76, 97, 107, 175–176,
219
in Ron Mahurin's stories, 154

pathetic, 193
in Martha Ringer's childhood, 198
in Del Ringer's stories, 76, 84, 153,
171, 203, 219
in Delbert Wick's stories, 110, 111–
112

I

Idaho County Voices, 113, 146n2–
146n3, 180n1
Idaho State Historical Society
Chief Joseph, 82*ph*
Nez Perce women, 71*ph*
identities, in personal stories, 220
Indian Camp at Slate Creek, in 1877,
70*ph*
"Indian Scare, The" (Brown), 191–192
"Indian War" (Mahurin, A.), 135–137,
148n8
"Indian War, The" (Ringer, D.), 78–82,
148n8
Indians (Nez Perce)
and attitudes toward, 178
battle at White Bird Hill (ID), 136,
147n8–148n8, 152, 152*ph*
boots, 70
Chief Joseph, 69, 78, 81–84, 82*ph,*
84, 84*ph,* 147n8–148n8
Chief White Bird, 147n8–148n8
Colville reservation (WA), 84
Indian War, the, 13–14, 17, 78–84,
135–138, 148n8, 150
moccasins and gloves, making, 70,
192
and Mrs. Benedict, 138*ph,* 146n5
Peter Mox Mox, 71, 74–75, 77
Reserve, 131
squaws, 71*ph,* 187, 192
indirect dialogue, 107, 141, 216
individual style, 8, 219
interior monologue, 192, 199, 216
Irishman (Edward Victor Robie), in
"The Indian War" story, 80–82,
135–138, 146n2

irony, use of
in Gus Carlson's stories, 165
in humor, 76, 97, 107, 175–176,
219
as literary device, 8, 216
Irwin, Dick, 160, 180n1
Irwin, Isaac, 160, 180n1

J

Jewett, Bill "Old Bill"
burnt house, 152, 154
disappearance of mother, 139–141,
210
and lady's choice dance, 53
red whiskers of, 4, 219
and the roofing, 193
roofing, the log house, 55–57
saddling a mule, 54
and Delbert Wicks, 106
Jewett, Preston. Jr. (daughter), 140–141
Jewett, Preston "Old Man Jewett"
death of, 58, 139, 209
grave of, 142ph
rattlesnake bite killing, 141
and rheumatism, 177–178
roofing, the log house, 55–60
Jewett, Rose "Old Lady Jewett," 53
and death of husband, 58, 139, 209
disappearance of, 139–141, 210
grave of, 141
headstone of, 142ph
"Jewetts, The" (Mahurin, A.), 139–141
"Jewett's Red Whiskers" (Ringer, D.), 4
"Jewett's Roof" (Ringer, D.), 55–57,
142
"Jewett's Saddle" (Ringer, D.), 54, 112
"John Kimbrough Gets Hired"
(Carlson), 164–165
"John Kimbrough's Death" (Robie),
118–119
"John Phelan Goes to Walla Walla"
(Carlson), 172–176
Johnson, Ronnie, 152–153

jokes, 24, 98, 111, 112, 144, 155. *see
also* humor
Jones, Seth, 38
Joseph, chief of the Nez Perce Indians,
69, 78, 81–84, 82ph, 84, 84ph,
147n8–148n8
Juliette (ID), 140

K

Kanky, Bob, 48–50
"Kanky and the Mules" (Ringer, D.),
48–50, 222
Kansas City (MO), 3
Kimbrough, John, 117–119, 117ph,
160, 177, 179, 217
death of, 209
and Gay Robie, 159
as sheepherder, 164–165
Kirkwood, Charlotte M., 147n8–148n8
Kirkwood, Mrs., 148
kittens, 198
Kowsky, Louie, 118

L

Labov, William, 11n4
Lake Patterson (WA), 26
Lap Wai (ID), 74, 131
Large, Mary Purcell, 20, 131–132,
146n3, 205
Large, Samuel "Sam," 131–132, 146n3
Large Bar, mine at (Slate Creek, ID),
132
leaking roof, 55–57
Lewiston (ID), 16, 19, 25
Lewiston Hill (ID), 16ph
lightning, 209, 211
"Lightning Kills Virgil" (Mitchell),
199–200
lines
descriptive, 141
of interior monologue, 189–190
punch, 111, 155

White Bird Hill Indian battle site, 152,
    152*ph*
White Bird Ridge (ID), 160
Wicks, Delbert, 109*ph*
    background of, 103–106
    "Bear, The," 108–109
    and Gus Carlson's style, 163
    on Chief Joseph, 69
    death, stories about, 209
    death of, 113n3
    description of Gus Carlson, 159
    dialogue, recounting scenes through,
        216
    and his dog (Bennett), 105*ph*
    on John Kimbrough, 117
    meeting with, 6
    "Muddy River," 111–112
    "Old Hollenbeak," 106–107, 113n1
    oral presentation, 217
    and rattlesnake stories, 109–110
    and Del Ringer's style, 109–110,
        112
    and Gay Robie's style, 122, 125
    stories, content of, 217
wild creatures, 58–60, 63–68, 104,
    108–110, 112
"windy stories," definition if, 3
woman's styles, 190, 222
Women's Club, in Parker (ID), 92
Wood, John, 146
Wyatt, Blanche, 46
Wyatt, Frank "Old Man Wyatt," 16–17,
    31, 32*ph,* 37, 45–49, 52n1, 154,
    156
Wyatt, Harry, 46
Wyatt, Margaret Ellen Conne, 45

RINGER-HARRAH FAMILY TREE

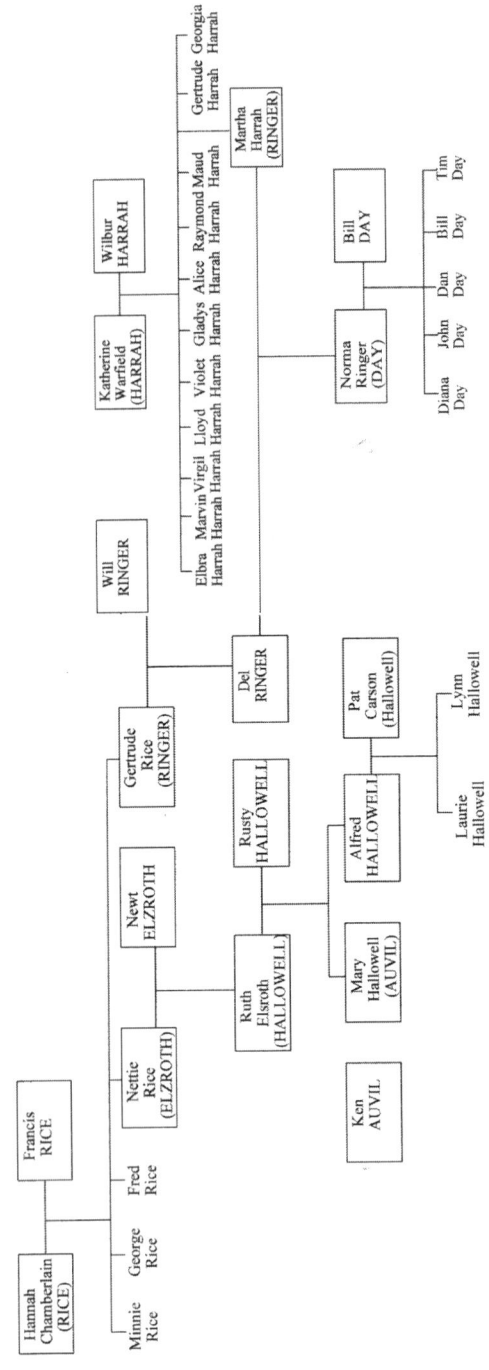

ROBIE FAMILY TREE

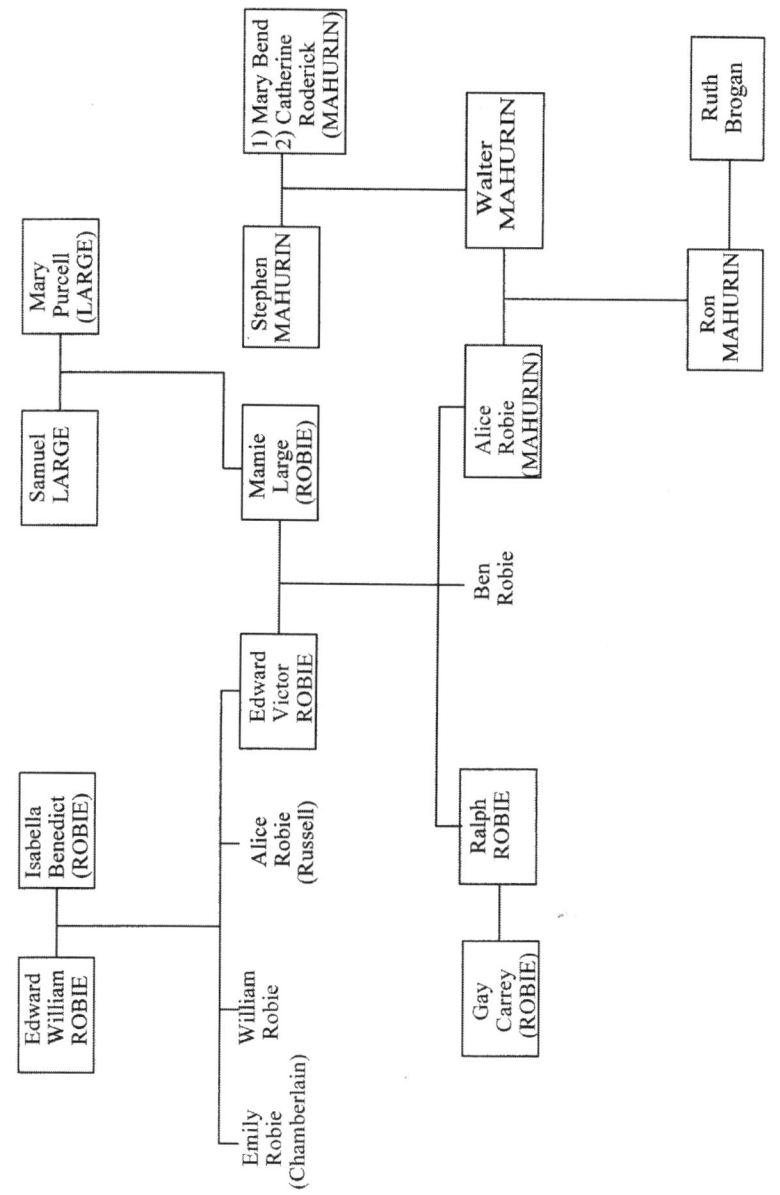

Map of Area

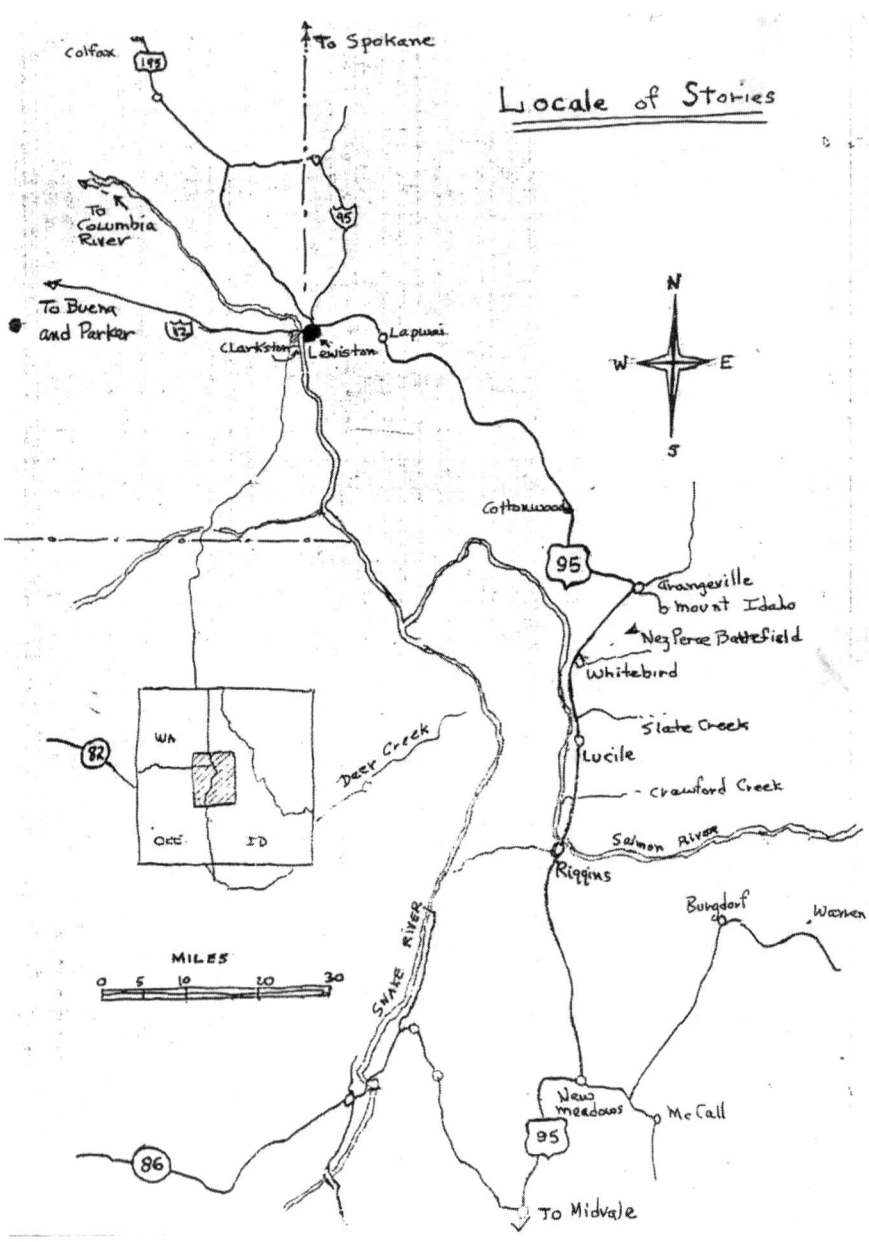

Made in the USA
Middletown, DE
22 October 2015